PUFFIN BOOKS

SUPER GRAN IS MAGIC

Mr Black's latest invention seemed harmless enough
– just a small black box that looked like a cross between a camera and a pocket calculator. But it was
lethal, because it was a *Hypnotizer*, giving its owner
the ability to hypnotize any person or wild animal
at the press of a switch!

Not that Super Gran was all that bothered: what
could a mere machine do that somebody *Super* like
her couldn't? But suddenly Super Gran had to get
interested because an unscrupulous stage magician
called Mystico planned to trick her out of the Hypnotizer in an attempt to improve his hopeless act. And
once he'd got hold of it, Super Gran and her Super-
powers would soon be in *his* power – and in the great
new show that would make his fortune . . . !

This is the fourth of Super Gran's marvellously
funny and exciting adventures. Also published in
Puffin are *Super Gran, Super Gran Rules OK!* and *Super
Gran Superstar.*

Forrest Wilson

SUPER GRAN

is Magic

Illustrated by David McKee

PUFFIN BOOKS

To (super) grans – everywhere

Puffin Books, Penguin Books Ltd, Harmondsworth, Middlesex, England
Penguin Books, 40 West 23rd Street, New York, New York 10010, U.S.A.
Penguin Books Australia Ltd, Ringwood, Victoria, Australia
Penguin Books Canada Ltd, 2801 John Street, Markham, Ontario, Canada L3R 1B4
Penguin Books (N.Z.) Ltd, 182–190 Wairau Road, Auckland 10, New Zealand

First published 1983

Copyright © Forrest Wilson, 1983
Illustrations copyright © David McKee, 1983
All rights reserved

Made and printed in Great Britain by
Cox and Wyman Ltd, Reading
Filmset in Monophoto Baskerville by
Northumberland Press Ltd, Gateshead

Contents

1   Mystico, Margo – and Magic Ian!

'Ladies and gentlemen ... boys and girls ... I have pleasure in presenting, for the very first time at a Muttlin's camp – Super Gran ... !' announced Mike, the compère at Muttlin's Holiday Centre, Slackpool.

The chief Marooncoat stepped back into the wings of the little theatre as Super Gran stepped forward to the centre of the stage to begin her performance.

'What? Who?' muttered Margo, who had just come off stage after doing *her* act and was waiting in the wings. 'A little old lady? On the stage? What does *she* do – demonstrate flower-arranging or something?'

'I'd like to start,' Super Gran told the Saturday-night audience, her first audience of the new week, 'by tearing a telephone directory in half ... !'

'Huh? What? Oh yeah? You're joking!' they murmured. Like Margo, the audience thought that Super Gran was having them on.

'And then,' Super Gran grinned, 'after that I'll tear *two* telephone directories in half – at the same time!'

'Okay, what's the gimmick? What's the joke?' Margo wondered, a smirk of disbelief on her face.

But the smirk instantly left her face to be replaced by a look of utter amazement when the little old, frail-looking, white-haired lady in the green and red floral

dress, lilac cardigan and tartan tammy proceeded to do exactly as promised – she lifted a thick telephone directory off a table and she tore it in half!

'Wow!' said the almost speechless Margo. 'Cr-rumbs . . . !'

'Och, that was nothing!' Super Gran told the applauding audience – as she lifted the other *two* directories off the table! 'But I go through an awful lot of directories this way!'

And that, of course, was only the start of Super Gran's stage act. For, to Margo's astonishment, she continued to demonstrate her Super-strength – by hoisting above her head one of the largest men from the audience. Then she demonstrated her Super-eyesight, Super-hearing and mind-reading powers.

'Wow! Cr-rumbs . . . !' repeated Margo, realizing that Super Gran's mind-reading, at least – if not her *other* powers – was genuine. For she and Mystico performed a so-called 'mind-reading' act in which they used codes, and she could see that Super Gran didn't have to resort to that kind of trick. 'Wow!' she said again, in sheer admiration.

But while she watched the rest of Super Gran's demonstration, Margo kept glancing round to see if Mystico, her boss, had arrived yet. He was late. In fact, he was so late that he'd missed their spot in the first-house show.

Not that this had unduly bothered Margo, for it had given her a chance to go on stage by herself and do her solo act for once. And on this occasion she had chosen to try her hand – or rather her feet! – at tap dancing.

'The van must've broken down,' she murmured. 'Again! It's about time he got a new one. Or at least, a *newer* one.' She knew that he'd never be able to afford a *new* van, not with the way their career was going. For their career was careering downhill! 'I wonder if he'll turn up in time for the second house? If he doesn't, I'll try out my singing ...'

Meanwhile, outside, Mystico *was* turning up. His ancient wreck of a van chugged in through Muttlin's gateway, stopped briefly at the security gatehouse and then drove on, spluttering and sparking along the road and into the main square of the camp. Mystico put on the brakes and the van, shuddering violently, eventually stuttered to a halt – stopping within a few centimetres of the glass-fronted offices of the administration block!

Lifting a black top hat and a black cloak off the passenger's seat, Mystico climbed out. He placed the hat on his head and he addressed the first people he saw, a boy and girl who came hurrying round a corner and into the square, heading towards the theatre.

'Ah! Greetings, my little kiddie-winkies!' Mystico said, in what he imagined was a 'let's talk to the kids' kind of voice – which just made Willard and Edison cringe!

He tried to swing his magician's black cloak round in an exaggerated theatrical gesture, to put it round his shoulders – but he couldn't fasten it properly and it fell into a puddle! So he touched his black top hat to them instead, in salute, but he didn't raise it. He twirled his thin, upward-pointing, black, waxed moustache, then he stroked his small, black, goatee beard as he tut-tutted before bending to pick the cloak up.

The van had Mystico's name painted on both sides of it. It read – or rather, it *should* have read – MYSTICO THE MAGICIAN. But unfortunately, business being bad, he couldn't afford a good paint job and it hadn't been done very well, with the result that there were spaces between some of the letters.

Willard pointed to it and said to Edison: 'MY STICO, THE MAGIC IAN ...? What's a "stico"?'

'Yes,' Edison laughed. 'And who is "Magic Ian"?'

Mystico had another try at putting on his cloak, and after getting enveloped in it and struggling with it for a few minutes, he succeeded in fastening it. *Then* he threw it round with a theatrical flourish – but the clasp gave way and it fell into the puddle again!

'Curses! Badgers' bedsocks!' he swore, then smiled. 'Well, anyway ... er ... hello my little ones! *I* ...' – he paused for effect – '... am the great Mystico ...!'

'The Magic Ian ...!' giggled Willard, trying to hide his giggle behind his hand as he glanced at Edison, who was doing likewise.

'Who? What?' Mystico glared at them, his beard and moustache quivering.

'Ask him,' Edison whispered to Willard, 'if he's got a magical brother – called magical "Magic Al"!' She got a fit of the giggles.

'Tell me, kiddie-winkies,' the man in black went on, with what he fondly imagined was a friendly smile –

11

but which was more of a leer! – 'can you kindly direct me to this holiday establishment's theatrical premises? M'mm? Can you?'

Willard and Edison stared blankly at each other, so Mystico translated: 'Muttlin's theatre, in other words?' He put his cloak on once again and this time he managed to fasten the clasp.

'That's it over there,' said Willard, stifling his giggles and pointing to a garishly coloured red and blue building, two blocks away.

'Ah, thank you, thank you, my children! A thousand thanks . . . !'

'That's okay,' giggled Edison, 'the first two'll do!'

'Now – you two teeny-weenies can render me a favour,' said Mystico.

He opened the rear doors of his rusty van and revealed his magical gear: a glittery table, boxes, cabinets, a bird-cage, a magic wand, packs of large-sized playing cards, sprays of imitation flowers, dozens of coloured handkerchiefs, ropes, scissors and other odds and ends. And there were also a couple of suitcases and bags nearer the front of the van.

'You can help me carry my props into the theatre,' Mystico said. It wasn't so much a request as an order.

'Oh . . . eh . . . er . . . well . . .' said Willard. 'You mean, from here?' He wondered why the man didn't just *drive* the van that short distance to the theatre.

But the truth was, if Mystico had driven the van he would have had to apply the brakes as soon as it *moved*, to make sure that they worked in time to stop the van again at the theatre!

'Oh, come on,' said Edison, nudging Willard towards the van. 'Let's help Magic Ian. We're going there anyway.'

So they carried most of Mystico's equipment to the theatre's stage-door, at the side of the building. That is, Willard and Edison carried it – for Mystico was too much of a gentleman to carry his own gear!

'*I* am the great Mystico,' Mystico announced to the stage-doorman – as if *that* explained everything!

'Better known as Magic Ian!' Edison giggled to Willard.

Mystico added, when the man merely stared at him blankly: 'I am in the show ... I'm late ... !'

'Well why didn't you say so?' the man grumbled, opening the door to admit them. 'But who are they?' He gestured towards Willard and Edison.

'They,' replied Mystico grandly, 'are my new, junior, temporary assistants.'

'Oh well, I dunno ...' began the man, but Edison interrupted him.

'Oh, it's okay. We've come to see Super Gran and we've got permission to go backstage,' she said, using the correct term to impress the man.

The doorman gestured them through and they walked along a short corridor to Mystico's dressing-room. They deposited his props on the table and on their way out they passed Margo, on her way in.

'Thank you my children, thank you, thank you. I shall

be eternally grateful to you ...' gushed Mystico, as Margo closed the door behind them.

Then she began, at once, to enthuse about an act she had just seen: 'Wow! You should've seen her ...'

But Mystico wasn't listening. He had other things on his mind.

'She's got Super-strength and Super-sight ...'

Mystico was too busy with his own list – a list of excuses for missing the first-house performance. 'Cor, blimey! That rotten old van broke down ...'

'And she's got X-ray eyesight and Super-hearing ...'

'And I'd to stop for a meal on the motorway – well, not actually *on* the motorway, you understand!' He laughed at his joke. 'At a service area café ...'

'And she can read your mind – and I mean *really* read your mind, not just code-words, and ...'

'And I'd to phone old Greenway, my agent, to see if he had any more work for us. But things are bad, they're pretty bad, and ...'

So neither person was actually listening to the other!

However, Margo persevered! 'I was speaking to her after she finished her performance, Mystico. She was telling me she's been here a week already and she's going to be touring another *three* Muttlin's camps after Slackpool.'

'Oh? Yeah?' Mystico wasn't really listening. He had too many problems of his own to listen to the details of one of his fellow artistes.

'Yeah,' Margo continued. 'She's going from here

down south to Tornmouth, then along the coast to Beastbourne, then up to Tarborough to finish off.'

'Is that so?' Mystico *still* wasn't listening. He took off his top hat and cloak, then he gingerly removed his thin, black, waxed moustache and his beard. 'Boy! These itch something chronic! And I've been *itching* to get them off!' He laughed.

'Mystico, why can't *we* get bookings at those places?' Margo asked. 'Huh? Why couldn't *we* have moved on to Tornmouth and Beastbourne and Tarborough?'

'M'mm? What's that . . . ?'

He had a vague idea that Margo had been chattering on about some little old lady or other. But he wasn't interested in listening to backstage gossip about little old ladies. To Mystico, all little old ladies looked the same and he reckoned that if you'd seen and heard about one of them, you'd seen and heard about the lot!

But of course he couldn't have been more wrong. For Super Gran certainly wasn't just any little old lady. Super Gran was different. *She* was unique.

If he had listened to Margo and paid more attention to her, he would have had his good idea sooner. But he didn't listen to her.

The trouble with 'Mystico the Magician' was that he wasn't *much* of a magician. He had never really been much good and he was even worse now. The older he got, the worse he got. He could no longer fool anyone – if he ever *could*! – with his sleight of hand, where the magician's hand is supposed to be quicker than the audience's eye. For in *his* case – *everyone's* eye was quicker than his hand!

'I have a length of ordinary rope here,' he'd tell his audience, 'and I'm going to cut it in half with these scissors. And then I'll say the magic words and – hey presto! – the ends of the rope will be miraculously joined together again!' But instead, the rope not only remained in two parts – the scissors fell into two parts as well!

He had therefore turned, in desperation, to other stunts – like his 'mind-reading' act. But it was not the *real* kind of mind-reading that Super Gran did, where she really and truly read people's minds. No, Mystico's was merely a trick, in which he and Margo used code-words.

Mystico, in the audience, would take an object from someone and would ask Margo, blindfolded on stage: 'What am I *holding here*, in my *hand*?' 'Holding' stood for 'lady's', 'here' stood for 'gold' and 'hand' stood for 'wrist-watch'. So Margo should have put the three words together to get the answer: 'A lady's gold wrist-watch ...!' – convincing the audience that Margo and Mystico were marvellously mysterious! But this happened only on rare occasions – because unfortunately Margo had a very bad memory!

And so, between Mystico's bad conjuring and Margo's bad memory, they found they were getting less and less work in the theatre. This engagement at the Slackpool Muttlin's was their last job in the foreseeable future – *and* they'd been lucky to get *it*.

Instead of working, Mystico spent more and more of

his time just trying to *find* work. And Mr Greenway, his agent, had told him repeatedly: 'Give yourself a shake, Mystico. Improve your act – or else you're finished!'

But Mystico, with superb self-confidence, had refused to listen to him until now – when the jobs had finally run out.

'I've applied for a job with a circus,' he told Margo. 'It's my only chance!'

But now it was *Margo's* turn not to listen to *Mystico*! For she was too busy with her *own* thoughts about her *own* stage career – without him. For the green-eyed, green-streaked, frizzy-haired blonde Margo was young and had ambitions of her own – and these didn't include her present boss.

Mystico realized that his assistant wasn't listening to him and decided, after all, to tell her nothing more about the circus job. He would go to the interview, and possible audition, on his own. And maybe he'd get the job more readily if *she* weren't tagging along and they thought that only *he* was looking for a job. And besides, the circus might not pay for an assistant.

So he said no more about his interview, which had been arranged for the Thursday afternoon of the following week, at two o'clock.

'Maybe,' he muttered, 'I'd better take a pack of cards with me. In case they want to see one of my tricks. Or should I take the rope and scissors? Oh no, perhaps not ... !'

'You know,' said Margo, suddenly emerging from her

daydream and looking closely at Mystico, 'you look quite different when you take your stage gear off. I mean your cloak and moustache and things. And that top hat makes you look heaps taller than you really are . . .'

2   The Hypnotizer

When Super Gran had agreed to tour four of the Muttlin's Holiday Centres in England she had asked if Willard and Edison could go with her.

'Yes, no problem,' the Muttlin's official told her. 'The girl can sleep in your chalet and we'll arrange an extra one for the boy.'

Then, a couple of days later, Edison had arrived at Super Gran's house with the news that her Dad wanted to see Super Gran and Willard.

'It's about his new invention,' Edison explained.

'You mean, the one I gave him some money to build?' said Super Gran. 'Out of the reward money I got for stopping yon stadium robbery up in Edinburgh?'

Edison nodded.

'And don't tell me,' Super Gran went on, frowning. 'He's working on another *new* invention – instead of making me another Super-machine?'

Edison nodded again.

Super Gran sighed resignedly. 'Right then, lassie, tell me – what great new invention has he invented *this* time?'

By now, Super Gran had stopped nagging Edison's Dad about the Super-machine. She had accepted that he was *never* going to go back to it again; that he was more interested in *new* inventions rather than his *old*, previous inventions. So that was that. There was no point in getting herself the name of being a nag over something like that.

'He wants to tell us all about it,' Edison said. 'Even *I* don't know what he's working on, but if you and Willard come over to our house tonight – all will be revealed!'

'And you don't know what it is?' Super Gran asked.

'No. All *I* know is it's a little black box – and it looks a bit like a camera.'

That evening Mr Black, in his wheelchair, lifted the little black box off his lap and held it up for everyone to see. Then he glanced briefly at Super Gran to see if she would make any comment about the Super-machine, but she didn't. She merely shrugged to show that she was resigned to the fact that he was working on something else.

'All right, laddie,' she sighed, 'what marvellous new machine have you got for us *now*? Eh?'

Mr Black leaned forward eagerly in his chair. Now that he had been spared his usual ticking-off about the Super-machine he could settle down, relax and tell them all about his fabulous new gadget. For Mr Black's new gadgets were *always* fabulous – at first!

He showed them the box, which looked like a cross between a camera and a pocket calculator! It was roughly fifteen centimetres long, seven centimetres broad and three centimetres deep. At the front there was an opening, similar to the lens on a camera. At the

top there was a row of four different-coloured lights. At the back, beside the row of coloured control buttons, there was a view-finder to aim through, also like a camera, and a mouthpiece, which was in fact a microphone.

'What *is* it?' Willard asked. 'And what does it *do*?'

'It's the Hypnotizer,' Mr Black informed them proudly. 'And it's for ... er ... um ... ah ... hypnotizing!'

'People?' asked Super Gran.

He nodded. '*And* animals.'

'Animals?' said Edison, surprised. 'Who'd want to hypnotize animals?'

'*You* would,' he told her, 'if they were wild and were attacking you!'

'Aye, I suppose you're right, laddie,' Super Gran agreed thoughtfully. 'I suppose a gadget like that *would* come in handy – for *ordinary* people, like *you* lot!' She drew herself up to her full height – which wasn't very high! 'But of course, for somebody *Super*, like *me* for instance – it's different! *I* wouldn't need that!'

Mr Black, ignoring Super Gran's boasting, leaned further forward in his chair, in his enthusiasm for his invention, until Edison thought he was going to fall out altogether!

'But it can be used for ever so *many* things,' he explained. 'For rounding up cattle and sheep, for breaking in and controlling wild horses. For training circus animals and controlling wild animals in zoos, or ones being transferred to other zoos. Not to mention animals that run amok and go berserk in public ...'

23

'Aye, well ... I see what you mean,' Super Gran admitted, interrupting him. 'I suppose it *would* be handy – for animals.'

'Ah, yes, but for people too,' Mr Black went on. He paused, then added: 'Criminals and terrorists ...'

'Where? Where ... ?' Super Gran, her hands shooting automatically into their karate-ready position, swung round towards the door. She seemed to be a bit disappointed *not* to see hordes of criminals and terrorists behind her!

'Och, I haven't had a good wee fight for ages now. I'm getting awful rusty, so I am. And ... ah ... er ... I was just trying out my reflexes, you understand!'

Mr Black laughed. 'Well the Hypnotizer would be just the thing to use on criminals and terrorists – for ordinary people, that is! Not that *you* would need it, Super Gran! We all know that!'

'Show us how it works. Give us a demonstration,' said Willard, who was fed up with all the talking and wanted some action.

But he wasn't going to see any. Not just then, in Edison's house. For Mr Black wasn't going to try it out on people. Not yet.

'I won't hypnotize any of you, but I *can* show you how it works,' he said.

He pressed the 'on' button and the white light on top of the Hypnotizer came on, to show that the machine was operating. Then he held it up as if he were taking a photograph with a camera and, looking through the view-finder, he aimed at the far wall of the room.

He pressed a second button and an amber light came on.

'That means the hypnotizing beam is working,' he explained. 'You can't *see* it. And you can't *hear* it, even though it's a sound wave, for it's an ultra-sonic one. Anyway, the beam's shooting out of the Hypnotizer and hitting the wall. So if someone was standing there he'd be under the influence of the machine by now and would be waiting to obey my command.'

'Wow!' said Willard. 'And how do you give the commands?'

Mr Black pointed to the microphone's mouthpiece. 'I just press this button, speak in here, tell the ... er ... victim what to do – and he does it! Just like that!'

'Are you *sure*, Dad?' Edison said doubtfully.

'Ah, well now, that's what I don't exactly *know*,' he confessed. 'I haven't tried it out yet, have I? But it *should* work okay.'

'How *does* it work?' Willard asked, intrigued by it. 'It's so titchy!'

'But *everything's* titchy nowadays,' Mr Black said. 'It's all those micro-chips, isn't it? You get micro-chips everywhere!'

'As long as you don't get micro-chips with your fish and chips!' Edison said.

'Well anyway, when I speak into it,' said Mr Black, going on with his explanation, 'the sound of my voice gets converted inside the Hypnotizer to an ultra-sonic wavelength and when the commands are passed out to the ... um ... victim – they're silent. So no one –

neither he nor anyone else standing near by – should hear them.'

'And that's all it takes to hypnotize someone?' Super Gran said. 'As easy as that?' Mr Black nodded. 'But it wouldn't hypnotize *me* as easily as that, would it? Not someone *Super*, like *me*?' She didn't like the idea that a small gadget like that could hypnotize *her*. For that would put her under the influence, and in the power, of someone else – which she didn't like the sound of.

'Yes,' Mr Black said, 'but not at *that* strength. That's what these different coloured buttons are for. For different signal-strengths, for different people. I'd press this blue one here for a child. And this pink one for an adult. And for a really strong person . . .'

'Like *me*? Super Gran?' said Super Gran.

Mr Black nodded. 'Yes, like you. For you I'd have to press this purple one, for full strength.'

'How long do the effects last, Dad?'

'About an hour or so, probably. Of course, there's also a reverse button – there . . .' He pointed to it. 'So that a person can be *un*-hypnotized, brought out of the trance, quite easily if need be. Then the red light comes on.'

'It's like a miniature set of traffic lights!' joked Edison.

'And what's it *like* to be hypnotized with the Hypnotizer?' Willard asked.

'Well the . . . er . . . victim won't know he's *being* hypnotized,' Mr Black explained. 'And he'll probably remember nothing about it afterwards.'

'To think that wee gadget could actually hypnotize

26

me!' Super Gran exclaimed, thinking again about it. She just couldn't get over it!

'Don't worry!' Mr Black said. 'There's no chance of *me* hypnotizing *you*!'

'Havers! I should hope not, laddie, I should hope not!'

Hypnotizing Super Gran indeed! What was the world coming to?

'Hey, talkin' about wild animals and zoos and things,' Willard said. 'Did you hear about Tub?'

'*Super* Tub, you mean?' Super Gran reminded him. 'No, what about him? Have they put *him* into one? A zoo, I mean!' She laughed.

'No, he's got a job in a circus and it's tourin' all round the country. And guess what . . . ?'

'What . . . ?' the others chorused.

'He's goin' to Slackpool with them – when *we're* there. Maybe he'll get us compli . . . complimen . . . compliment . . . er, I mean . . . free tickets to it, huh?'

Mr Black looked thoughtful. 'A circus, eh? With lions and tigers . . . ?'

'What are you thinking, Dad?' Edison saw the glint in his eye.

He snapped his fingers. 'That's it! That's how we can try out the Hypnotizer. The very thing!'

'What – on Tub?' said Willard.

'No! On the wild animals in his circus,' Mr Black explained. 'It would be ideal to try it out on animals.'

'But I thought you said it *did* work on animals?' Edison said.

'Well, yes – in theory. But – I told you – I haven't

tried it out yet. Oh, I'm sure it'll work on them okay. Trust me!'

'Humph! Trust *you*?' snorted Super Gran. 'What about the Super-machine – it blew up! And the Shield – it shattered! And the Skimmer . . . !'

'*It* got pinched,' Mr Black interrupted. 'Well, that was hardly *my* fault. *I* didn't leave it lying around. And besides, they all *worked* okay – at least, to begin with!'

'Oh, let's give it a try, Gran, eh?' said Willard eagerly.

'We'll contact Tub and see if he can arrange something, shall we?' said Edison.

'Sure! Why not!' Super Gran agreed. She was always willing to accept a challenge. She'd try anything once.

And so, a few weeks later, now that they were actually *in* Slackpool, they paid a visit to Tub's circus – with the complimentary tickets that Willard had hoped for! – and had a few words with him after the show.

'Thursday'll be the best day,' he told them. 'Cos everyone's having the afternoon off. They're all going to a circus wedding. Our bearded lady and india-rubber man are getting married.'

'But aren't *you* going, Tub?' Edison asked.

Tub shook his head.

'Aw, you've not been invited?' Edison said, all sympathetic.

'I'm not bothered,' Tub assured her. 'I've just started with the circus and I don't really know them anyway. And besides, *someone's* got to stop here and look after the place. So I said *I'd* do it.' His face brightened as he added: 'As long as they fetch me back a bit of wedding cake, that's all ... !'

'So we can all sneak in here *then*?' said Willard. His eyes lit up as he looked round the Big Top.

'It's not exactly sneaking in,' Edison pointed out, 'if there's nobody here to stop us!'

'But can you arrange to have lions or tigers or something here, for Mr Black to practise on?' Super Gran asked Tub.

'Yeah, no problem,' he assured her. 'I've been giving Tamo, the lion-tamer, a hand and I've got to know a bit about lion-taming. I'll get them out of their cages into the big cage, don't worry.' He was referring to the large cage which was brought into the Big Top for the lions' performance in the show. 'Cos we'll have it in here for the morning practice anyway, see?'

'Then all we've got to do now,' Super Gran said, 'is to phone Edison's Dad and tell him to come up here on Thursday afternoon ... ?'

'And remind him to bring the Hypnotizer with him!' laughed Edison.

So it was all arranged. Mr Black would come to Slackpool for the day with the Hypnotizer and they would all go up to the Sirius Circus, which was situated in a field next door to Slackpool's Scanley Park. And Tub would introduce them – and the Hypnotizer – to the lions.

'I ... I suppose,' said Edison thoughtfully and hesitantly, 'that it'll be safe enough? With the lions, I mean?' She suddenly looked worried.

'Don't panic. They'll be *inside* the cage and we'll be *outside*,' Tub assured her. 'At least, *you'll* all be. I mean ...' He puffed out his chest, proudly. '*I* might go inside, with me being a bit of a lion-tamer, that is. But you'll all stop outside. Don't worry.'

'And besides,' Super Gran added, grinning, '*I'll* be here too, just in case anything *does* go wrong. Och, don't worry, lassie! What *can* go wrong, eh? What can possibly go wrong ... ?'

3   Breakers on the Beach!

Two days before they were due to try out the Hypnotizer on the lions, Super Gran and company decided
to spend some time on the Slackpool beach. Or at least,
two of them had decided! Edison wanted to do something
else!

'I want to go and see Scanley Park for a change,'
she said. 'We've been down to the beach already.'

'Yeah,' Willard agreed, 'but this time we're goin' to
play football on the sand . . .' He bounced his new football on the prom.

It was a special new football. It was autographed by
Kenny Keegan, the famous international star, Willard's
hero.

'Well, *I'm* not playing football, that's for sure!' Edison
replied haughtily. 'That's all you two ever think about
– playing football! Humph!'

'Och well, lassie, I haven't played with Willard for
a while. And he keeps on pestering me . . . er, I mean
. . . trying to persuade me to have a wee game with him.
It's just a *wee* game on the beach, we won't be long.
You can come and watch if you like. If you're *sure* you
don't want to join in . . . ?'

'No *thank* you! I'd rather go for a ride on one of those
open-top tramcars – if I'm not to get to Scanley Park,

that is! I might as well have a trip along the prom and see the sights.'

'Well, see that you have a trip *on* a tram, and not in *front* of one!' said Willard, knowing that Edison was liable to trip over her own two feet!

'Humph!' she snorted, looking to see if there was a tram coming.

In Slackpool the trams ran along the sea-front, between the prom and the beach on the one side and the shops of the town on the other. And they ran past Muttlin's Holiday Centre, the piers, the miles of golden sand and the famous Slackpool Tower which dominated the whole of the sea-front.

'Listen lassie,' Super Gran suddenly said, 'have you got yon walkie-talkie gadget with you?'

'You mean my CB radio? Yes, I have! *He* keeps making me carry it about with me!' Edison complained, gesturing towards Willard. 'And I can't make head nor tail of it!' She took the radio out of her pocket, looked at it and shook her head, puzzled. 'Why do you ask?'

'Well I thought,' Super Gran said, 'that after we've played football maybe Willie could call you up on *his* set. Then we can all arrange to meet and go up to Scanley Park together. How about that?'

'Yeah, well all right,' Edison said grudgingly. '*If* I can make out what he's talking about, that's all!'

Before coming to Slackpool, Willard had kept going on and on, for weeks, about wanting a CB radio, the same as all his pals had. So just before they left home Mr Black took pity on him and made him not *one*

32

walkie-talkie, portable CB radio transceiver set – but two. One for him and one for Edison, so that they could talk to each other on them.

The sets were quite small – seven centimetres long, six centimetres broad and two centimetres deep. They fitted together into a special carrying case – roughly the size of the Hypnotizer – when they weren't being used. And when they were being used Edison carried hers in a pocket of her jeans or tee-shirt, while Willard usually kept his in the carrying case, which was made of black plastic and hung on a strap round his neck.

Willard thought at first that the radio was fantastic. It was as good as the ones his pals had, only much smaller and much more powerful. Where his pals' sets had a range of only about half a mile, Mr Black's sets had a range of about three miles.

But, as with most of his inventions – sooner or later – there was a snag! He had, somehow or other, managed to build a fault into them – they could communicate only with each other! No one else, apparently, could tune into their wavelength. Which was all very well if Willard and Edison wanted to speak only to each other and no one else – but after a while they got fed up with this and yearned to hear someone else's voice coming over the airwaves! *Anyone's*!

But the real trouble, as far as Edison was concerned, was that Willard would insist on using CB radio jargon – the kind of slang talk that lorry drivers and other CB radio users used. Things like:

'Do you read me, good buddy? Crank us your handle.

33

There's a breaker on the side. Ten-nine. Ten-four. Roger and out . . .' Which meant:

'Do you understand me, fellow CB radio user? Give your name. There's another CB user waiting to come in on our conversation. Please repeat your message. Okay. Message received, stop speaking.'

But Edison couldn't understand all this and it seemed too complicated to remember. 'And besides,' she'd say, 'why can't you just speak plain English? You know there's nobody else going to answer you anyway! Just *me*!'

She reckoned it was silly of Willard to use CB slang when only *she* could hear him – and couldn't understand him anyway!

Hence her reluctance to carry her radio everywhere she went – especially as Willard kept bullying her into taking it about with her, just because *he* took *his* everywhere with *him*!

'I know how you feel about it, Edison,' Super Gran said. 'But this time it'll come in handy. To contact you and arrange to meet somewhere.'

'Yeah, that's a good idea, Gran,' Willard said as he bounced his football.

'Oh, well, I suppose it is,' Edison agreed grudgingly. 'Oh! Here's a tram coming! I'm off to catch it!'

So, while Super Gran and Willard went down the flight of steps from the prom to the sand to try out Willard's new ball, Edison hurried to the nearest tram-stop to catch the open-topped tramcar which was approaching.

At first Super Gran and Willard played football by

34

themselves. But it wasn't long before a dozen other boys – and girls! – joined in and played with them. After all, it isn't every day of the week that you get the chance – or the novelty! – of playing football with a little old lady! And especially one who could play football the way *this* little old lady could play!

'Come on, kids, can you not do better than that?' she yelled, as she dribbled the ball past half a dozen of them, weaving her way in and out of them as if she were just about to score the winning goal in the World Cup!

'Whew! She's too fast for *me*,' muttered one boy, sitting down for a rest!

'Jings!' she exclaimed. 'I could beat the lot of you with my eyes shut and my feet tied together! Come on, what's keeping you?'

She gave the ball a hefty kick – and a certain little white poodle, sniffing around a sand-castle which a child had just made, suddenly took to its heels!

Super Gran got possession of the ball again and fought her way through the throng of children trying to take it from her. 'Here, Willard,' she called, 'take the pass ...' as she kicked it over the children's heads towards him.

But the trouble was – she forgot her own strength! She gave it such a Super-hefty kick this time – a super Super-kick! – that it flew up in the air, over *all* their heads, away from the beach and up on the prom. And even on the prom it was still up in the air. So where it landed ... Well, she just didn't *know* where it landed. She, and the children, lost sight of it!

'Oh-oh!' she cried, as she started to run after it.

'Hey! That's my new ball!' yelled Willard. 'My special Kenny Keegan ball! Where's it gone? It'll get run over – or nicked . . . !'

The thought that a tram's wheels might cut it in half was enough to make Willard extremely agitated. Or, even worse, that someone might lift it and run off with it, thinking that it was a gift from heaven. (Not so much 'pennies from heaven', as 'Kenny's from heaven'!)

'Okay! Don't panic, I'll get it!' Super Gran yelled back over her shoulder to him as she raced towards the prom steps. 'Never fear – Super Gran's here!'

She ran across the sand, dodging the mass of adults and children who were sitting about on deck-chairs, pic-nicking behind wind-breaks and lying on the beach, sun-bathing; some of them she leapt over, rather than taking the longer way round them! Then she'd to jump over youngsters building sand-castles and making sand-pies, then get past lots of people – toddlers to grannies – stuffing themselves with ices, crisps, chips, hamburgers, candy-floss and lollipops. Then she'd to dodge past people playing sand-cricket, tennis and badminton; not to mention a variety of joggers. And then she'd to leap up the steps to the prom, three at a time, but avoiding collisions with others going up or coming down. And, especially on sand, all this took time – even for Super Gran, going as fast as she could.

So by the time she reached the prom, the ball was nowhere in sight. It had disappeared. So what had hap-pened to it? *Had* somebody stolen it?

37

She spent some time looking in the immediate area. She peeked into a couple of nearby tram-shelters and under a kiosk. Then she peeked under a couple of seats on the prom – much to the annoyance of the people who were sitting on them! Finally, having no success, she retraced her steps down to the beach and wandered slowly across the sand to tell Willard, who would be disgruntled, that his new Kenny Keegan ball was lost, or stolen. And it was all her fault.

But as she approached the crowd of children clustered around Willard, and they fell away to let her through, she saw that he was grinning – and he shouldn't have been! He should have been sad, or angry, or annoyed. But he was grinning! And he had his CB radio to his ear.

'Huh?' she exclaimed. He was certainly taking his loss in good part and didn't seem to be bothering about it.

'It's okay – don't worry – listen ...' And he handed the set to Super Gran.

She put it to *her* ear.

'Hello – Roger?' said Edison's voice. 'Ten-four ...'

'There aren't any Rogers here!' grinned Super Gran. 'This is Super Gran and it's not ten-four!' She laughed and looked at her watch. 'It's one-thirty!'

'Out, good buddy breaker, and Roger. No ... ah ... er ... I mean ...' Edison went on, thoroughly confused. 'Oh, it's *you*, Super Gran? Thank goodness. I can stop speaking that daft CB language now it's *you* and not Willard on the line.'

'Aye, just you go ahead and speak English, lassie. We *all* speak that.'

38

'Yes, well – *some* of us do!' retorted Edison, referring to Super Gran's Scottish accent.

'Now, lassie . . . !'

'Only joking, Super Gran!' Edison said. 'Well anyway, I was just asking Willard if you two had lost something?'

'Lost something?' Super Gran, for the moment, was puzzled. Then she remembered. 'No, not me . . . oh, you mean the footb – but how did *you* know? Don't tell me *you've* got some of my Super-powers? That *you* can read minds?'

Edison laughed. 'No, not really. It's just that I've got the ball here with me. On the tram. That's what I was telling Willard.'

'With you? But how *can* you have, lassie?' She turned and looked at Willard, who was having a quiet giggle to himself.

'The tram I caught only went along the prom a short distance to the pier, then it turned and went back the way it came, past the Tower,' Edison explained. 'And while I was sitting here, minding my own business – on the top deck, the *open*-top deck! – a football suddenly appeared out of the air and landed at my feet. But it's not an ordinary football – even *I* could see that! It's a special one – with Kenny Keegan's autograph on it!'

'So *that's* where it went!' Super Gran exclaimed, breaking into a smile. 'Whew! That's a relief! We thought it had been pinched.'

'The only thing is,' Edison continued over the radio, 'and I didn't tell Willard – you must've kicked it too hard! It's got a puncture! It's flat!'

'A puncture? Och, don't worry, we'll get it fixed – repaired – all right.'

'Humph! *I'm* not worrying!' snorted Edison. 'But it puts an end to your game of football, doesn't it?' Her voice brightened.

'What?' cried Willard. 'Punctured – the ball?'

His grin changed to a frown. So that was *another* game of football that he and Super Gran hadn't finished! He was fated! If Willard had an ambition in life, it was to finish – just once – a game of football with Super Gran!

'So that means,' Edison went on cheerily, 'that we can go up to Scanley Park now – and do something else apart from football, eh? It's *my* turn now to do what *I* want?'

'Aye, all right,' agreed Super Gran, nudging Willard in the ribs until he too nodded silently that he agreed. 'And Willard agrees too,' she added.

'Not to mention,' Edison continued, 'me getting Willard's precious ball back to him, too? Willard, do I hear you saying, "Thanks, Edison, for getting my ball back"?'

She didn't, of course, hear that! Not until Super Gran nudged Willard in the ribs again and he mumbled: 'Ouch! Er . . . thanks, Edison' – faintly and grudgingly!

'I'll jump off this tram and get the next one back and meet you on the prom. Okay?' said Edison. 'I'll sign off now, good buddies. Ten-three. Roger and out!'

'There,' said Willard, who heard this last bit. 'I *knew* it! She *does* know the CB codes . . .!'

After lunch Edison got her way: the three of them

40

went up to Slackpool's Scanley Park to see what *it* had to offer in the way of entertainment. And, as there was no point in taking Willard's punctured football with them, Super Gran bought them a frisbee.

They played putting, went on the boating-lake, played tennis and outdoor table tennis and then, near the tennis courts, they started to play with the frisbee. They threw it to one another for a while, until Willard asked his Gran how far she thought she could throw it.

'Oh, I could throw it miles!' she claimed, with her usual lack of modesty.

'Well don't throw it miles in *that* direction, Gran,' Willard said, pointing to a fenced-off area beside the park. 'Or it'll end up in Tub's circus, there!'

The side of the circus bordered on to the park, but its main entrance was in the road which ran past the park.

'No, but honestly, Super Gran,' Edison said. 'How far do you *really* think you could throw it?'

They were standing on the steps of the building which housed the tennis pay-desk and dressing-rooms and a café. And Willard and Edison were busily licking their third ice cream of the day as they challenged Super Gran.

'Yeah, let's see, Gran,' Willard urged her, with a slurp!

'All right, then . . .' She looked around the park, and pointed. 'See yon wee stone tower over there?' The little building was a fair distance away from them. 'I bet you I could reach *there* with it.'

'I bet you couldn't,' said Willard, with another slurp.

'I bet you I could,' Super Gran argued. 'It's easy-peasy!'

'Right, Gran,' said Willard, 'I'll bet you an ice cream you can't hit it. If you *do* hit it – then you buy me another ice! Okay?'

'Done!' said Super Gran, before realizing that it was she who'd been done! If she achieved the target she was aiming for, then *she* would have to pay Willard, and not the other way around as it should have been!

'Oh, go on,' she relented. 'I'm feeling generous today!'

She waited a few moments until there was no one in the way and then she threw the frisbee so that it curved away out to the right. It looked as though it was going to miss the little stone tower by a mile.

But then, as if by magic, the frisbee curved back in again at the last minute and hit the side of the stone structure with a 'clunk'.

'There! I *told* you I'd do it, didn't I? It was easy-peasy!' said Super Gran – but she was talking only to Edison. Willard had disappeared!

He was back inside the café, waiting for Super Gran to come in and pay for the ice cream he was ordering, to settle her 'lost' bet.

And that was his fourth ice that day, so far . . . !

4   Super Gran Gets a Proposal!

'Do *you* go on stage *before* Magic Ian, or after him?' Willard asked, as his Gran applied her stage make-up in her dressing-room that evening at Muttlin's.

'He's on first,' Super Gran replied. 'In fact, he's on right now, isn't he?' She turned to Edison, who nodded.

'And I don't think he's much good,' Edison remarked. 'Margo – that's his assistant, you know? – was telling me she wants to leave him. She wants to go on the stage . . .'

'Huh?' said Willard. 'But she *is* on the stage! She hands him his props and she reads people's minds, doesn't she? *That's* on the stage!'

'Yes,' Edison sighed, 'but she doesn't *mean* like that. She means going solo – on her own. As a singer or a dancer or an actress, or something. She wants to be a big star, not a conjuror's assistant all her life.'

'*I* wouldn't mind bein' a conjuror's assistant,' Willard enthused. 'Just think – you'd get to know how all those magic tricks are done . . .'

'Yes, but you'd look silly in Margo's short skirts!' Edison retorted.

Luckily, at that moment one of the stage-hands knocked on the dressing-room door, then stuck his head round to tell Super Gran that she was due on stage. So that prevented a retort from Willard to Edison!

To cut down on his own work and as practice for Margo, Mystico had now agreed to give her her own 'spot' in each show, and this time she had chosen to sing. So while Margo took the centre of the stage, Mystico retired to the wings to let her have the spotlight. And while Margo sang – 'screeched' would be a better word for it! – Mystico stood watching, his hands covering his ears.

As he stood there at one side of the stage, trying to shut out Margo's monotonous un-musical voice, he saw a little old lady appear in the wings at the other side of the stage, with those two kids who had helped carry his props the other day. Now what was *she* doing there, he wondered? Surely a little old lady like that wasn't going to perform on stage? What on earth could *her* act be, he wondered – a demonstration of flower-arranging, perhaps?

Margo's solo was a disco version of a Welsh song, which she had introduced as being 'a tribute to Wales'.

'Humph!' muttered Mystico, 'it's more like a tribute to "wails"!'

Margo finished – to *everyone's* relief! – and Mystico stepped back on to the stage to take his bow with her. Then the curtain closed, they stepped back off stage again and Mike, the Muttlin's compère, stepped forward.

'Ladies and gentlemen ... boys and girls ... may I present – Super Gran ... !'

Mystico was astonished to hear the polite but luke-

44

warm applause which had followed *his* act increase dramatically in volume to become tumultuous applause welcoming the little old lady as she stepped from the wings on to the centre of the stage.

'Huh?' he exclaimed from the wings, as he turned to see who was being applauded. 'They're applauding *her*?'

What could a little old lady like *that* do, he wondered? What talent could *she* possibly have, to warrant a welcome like that? And before she had actually *done* anything, too? He didn't realize that the audience had seen her previous performances – and were back for more of the same!

The audience had already seen and heard the other acts: the singers, dancers, comedians, pop groups and jugglers – which were all much of a muchness. If you'd seen one, you'd seen the lot, they reckoned. But Super Gran was different. She was unique. There just wasn't anyone else quite like her.

As Mystico continued to watch from the wings, Super Gran started her act by bending an iron bar into knots! Then, standing on a chair between two heavy, brawny men from the audience, she put an arm round each of them and lifted them both into the air!

Then, after the deserved applause had died down, she turned her attention to mind-reading. And of course, unlike Mystico, she really *did* read people's minds and didn't need an assistant and a 'code'. She did it all 'straight'.

Mystico was impressed – with *all* of her Super-powers. And suddenly he had his idea, his great idea. It came

to him in a flash, a bolt from the blue – like the blue flash which had turned the little ordinary old Granny Smith into Super Gran in the first place.

He dived off to find Margo in their dressing-room. He couldn't wait to tell her his fabulous idea.

'Margo – have you seen that little old lady out there? On stage? Doing her act? Little Mrs ... er ... Granny something-or-other ... ?'

'Super Gran?' Margo prompted.

'Yes, that's it. Super Gran! And she *is* super! Have you seen what she can do? You'll never believe it!' His eyes, glowing with excitement, were popping out of his head. 'She's got Super-strength and Super-sight and Super ...'

'Yes, I know,' Margo replied, calmly, as she removed her make-up. 'I told you about her before ...'

'And she's got X-ray eyesight and can read minds, and ...'

'Yes, I know. I *tried* to tell you about her before ...'

'And her mind-reading really *is* mind-reading! Not like ours ... !'

'But you wouldn't listen to me ...' Margo went on.

'She's great, terrific, super – that's what she is, Super ... !'

'And you're not listening to me now, either ... !'

And so it went on. He enthusing about *his* great new discovery. And she complaining that he never listened to her when she told him anything.

'I told you all about Super Gran the other day,' she

said – but he *still* wasn't listening! He was too busy revealing his great idea to her:

'Listen Margo, this is what we've been waiting for ...'

'What *you've* been waiting for, more like,' she muttered. '*I've* been waiting for my big break, for a talent-spotter to spot my talent – as a dancer, or a singer, or an actress, or a ...'

'Listen to me, Margo, will you?' he said. 'You *never* listen to me ...!'

'What? *I* never listen to *you*? Cheek! *You* never listen to *me*!'

'But this'll put us in the big time, Margo. The big show – what I've always dreamed about. Haven't I ever told you about it?'

'Yes – repeatedly!' she groaned.

'And *she* – Super Gran – could be the starting point. I could be famous. Just think of it: "Mystico the Magician's Magic Show – with Super Gran". And ... er ... of course, with Margo. The crowds'll flock in.'

For years now Mystico had been looking for something special, something different, for his act. Something which would make it famous and outstanding. Something which would have the audiences queueing up all the way round the theatre just to get in.

And he wouldn't have to worry, then, about where his next job was coming from. He wouldn't have to worry whether his agent got him work or not. He wouldn't need to look for theatre managers who would employ him – *they* would go down on their knees, and plead with him to work for them.

And all it would take to do this, the gimmick that he needed – was Super Gran. For, with her doing all her stunts, the audiences would clamour to see the shows.

'It shouldn't be too difficult,' he murmured, 'to get her to join me.'

And this, of course, would only be the start; the start of his really *big* ambition. For years now he had wanted to have his very own super stage show with all the grand illusions: sawing a woman in half, cabinets for making people disappear, levitating someone into the air, the Indian rope trick . . . !

'If only I could get started,' he went on. 'But I need a really good act to build the show on. And who better than – Super Gran?'

'M'mm? Super Gran,' muttered Margo. She wasn't really listening.

'She'll bring the crowds in and make me lots of money,' Mystico enthused, rubbing his hands together. 'I'll give her *some* of it, of course – not a lot, but *some*! And then, when I've made enough, I'll buy the equipment I need and hire the stage-hands and assistants I'll require to rig up all those big illusions – the *really* big illusions. Then I'll *really* be in the big time!'

Margo, since her latest successful – *she* thought! – solo spot in that evening's show, had been daydreaming about *her* ambitions and hadn't been listening all that much to Mystico. *Her* ambitions were going to take her into a career in show biz, in dancing, pop-singing, TV or films – she wasn't fussy which! And working for

Mystico was only the first small step towards this – she thought.

'I'm going to ask Super Gran to join me ... er ... us,' Mystico continued, 'in my ... er ... um ... our act. With all her Super-powers she'll be ...'

But Margo wasn't listening again. So Mystico left her gazing at her own reflection in the dressing-table mirror, daydreaming, as he went in search of Super Gran's dressing-room.

'Gran, it's Magic Ian!' said Willard in a loud voice, as he answered the knock on the door.

'Shhh! He'll hear you!' Edison shushed, but Willard merely shrugged.

Mystico entered the dressing-room, glared at Willard and introduced himself: '*I* am the famous Mystico, the magician ...'

'Magic Ian!' Willard repeated, by way of a translation.

Mystico glared at the boy again and touched his top hat, in salute to Super Gran, but didn't remove it. Then he bowed to her and, with a flourish of his cloak, he bent to kiss her hand. But the cloak swept round in front of him and he got rather entangled in it!

'Oh,' said Super Gran, with a grin, 'the famous Mystico?'

The man twirled his black moustache, stroked his black beard and smiled his crooked leer.

'Well, I'm the famous Super Gran!'

'Hum ... yes ... quite ... I *have* heard of you, of course,' he replied. 'And I am here, dearest lady, I assure you, with a proposal which I am certain ...'

'What? A proposal?' yelled Willard. 'For Gran? You want to marry Gran?' He was horrified at the very idea! Imagine having Mystico as a Granpa!

'No! Hum ... er ... I mean ...' stammered Mystico. 'I *should* say – a proposition. A business arrangement. Something which will be to our mutual advantage ...'

It was getting to be a bit of a strain trying to maintain a conversation using the large words which Mystico imagined his dignified image required. So he stopped trying and resorted to his usual everyday language:

'I'm offering you a job, dear. In my act. And I'll pay you, of course!'

He went on to give her some details of his show, but he didn't actually mention the salary he had in mind.

'Let me just see if I understand this, laddie,' Super Gran said. 'You're offering me a job in this great, new, super-duper, colossal, stupendous, fantastic magical show that you're organizing. Is that it?'

Mystico, who had made out that the show was almost ready to go on the road, nodded. And Super Gran didn't think to read his mind, to find out that he was exaggerating somewhat.

For, to tell the truth, she was tempted by his offer. There was nothing she would have liked better than to go up on a stage *every* night, instead of just for a few weeks in the summer at the Muttlin's Holiday Centres. If she could only get into some of the top theatres in the country and, in time, on to the telly, then her fame would *really* spread.

She was tempted. And especially when she heard what

Mystico was proposing – a big, lavish, grand, glittering, glamorous show being taken all round the country, then to London, then abroad – Europe, America, Australia . . .

Yes, she was certainly tempted. And so was Willard! For he was looking forward to getting away from school to go with her and assist her. And even Edison, briefly, got rather carried away with the thought of it – but not for long!

'Are you goin' to *do* it, Gran?' Willard asked eagerly. '*Are* you? And can *I* come with you? Huh? Huh, Gran?'

'*Are* you going to do it, Super Gran?' Edison echoed, doubtfully, by now already having second thoughts about it.

'Well? *Are* you?' Mystico demanded, getting edgy, impatient for her answer.

On his way along to her dressing-room he had been making plans for the show and was getting all enthusiastic about it. At the same time, he was on edge in case she turned him down, so he was slightly nervous while awaiting her decision.

'What do you say, eh? I'll put your name up in lights, you'll be famous . . .'

'But I *am* famous, laddie! Amn't I, kids?' She turned to the children.

'Yes,' agreed Mystico, 'but I mean *really* famous. *World*-famous! You're not *world*-famous yet, are you?'

'We-ell . . . no . . . not exactly . . . no, I can't say I am. Not *world*-famous . . .' she admitted. 'There are *still* a few people who haven't heard of me!' This fact puzzled – and peeved! – her somewhat.

'But you *will* be, after you join me in my show. I promise ...' He would have promised anything, just then, to get her to say yes. 'What's it to be, eh? What's your decision?' He twirled his moustache and stroked his beard.

'No ...'

'Pardon?'

'No, I don't think so, laddie. Thanks all the same.'

'What?' Mystico couldn't believe his ears. She had turned down his fabulous offer to star in his big, lavish, grand, glittering, glamorous show – which by now he had convinced *himself* was already in existence! 'But ... but why ...?'

'Well laddie, I'd *love* to join your stage act, I really would. But I'd just spend all my time showing off!'

'But you *like* showin' off, Gran!' Willard pointed out, not unreasonably.

'Aye, that's true, but ...'

'And you *do* spend a lot of time showin' off!' he went on, interrupting her again.

'Aye, that's true, too! But there are *other* things for me to do, apart from showing off. I've pledged to use my Super-powers for helping people. And fighting crime, when I have to.'

'But ... Super Gran ...' Mystico had another go at persuading her to re-consider, but she wouldn't. She was adamant. She had made up her mind and she wasn't going to change it. Not for anyone.

Mystico offered to double her salary – despite the fact that he hadn't actually mentioned what the salary would be in the first place! But she still refused.

Then Willard had a go: 'Aw, Gran – think how famous you'll be. Think of the fortune you'll make . . .' But Super Gran turned down *his* plea too.

Edison was the only one who didn't try to persuade her. For she knew that Super Gran wouldn't really be happy if she was only showing off every evening in a stage act, when she could be out and about, doing good turns and using her Super-powers to fight crime.

Mystico – eventually! – accepted that Super Gran wouldn't change her mind. So he slammed out of her dressing-room to go and tell Margo the bad news. And on the way there, in his temper, he yanked off his false beard and moustache – before he remembered that he shouldn't do it quickly!

'Ouch! Ow-wow!' he yelped.

His only hope now, without Super Gran, was the circus job. That, certainly, would tide him over for a *little* while, although how long *that* job would last, no one knew. It was all rather depressing.

No, on second thoughts, his only *real* hope was his great idea – getting Super Gran to join his act, leading to him starting up his big show. His face brightened, then set in a determined look. He resolved, there and then, to *get* her, somehow, to join him – although how, he didn't yet know.

But he'd get her, all right, by hook or by crook. By fair means, or foul . . . !

5   Lions Lyin' About!

When Mystico set off for his interview at the circus on the Thursday, he *still* had no idea how to persuade Super Gran to join his act. But he was hoping that something would turn up. And, as it turned out, something did!

He had phoned his agent again and had again been told that there was definitely no other work for him, so the circus job was his only hope. After lunch, he spluttered his way in the van to the field at the back of the town for his interview with Mr Mann, the circus manager.

Super Gran and company were also preparing for their visit to the circus, that afternoon, to test Mr Black's Hypnotizer while they had the place to themselves. Super Gran had agreed to give a special lunch-time performance at the theatre, so she told the others to go on ahead. 'I'll see you at the circus with Tub as soon as I can get away. Okay?'

But when she came out of the theatre she was mobbed by a crowd of admiring youngsters thrusting autograph books at her. Then, when she had managed to get away from them, she dashed out through the main gate to catch a tram along the prom to the Tower. But then she got held up, 'blethering' – as *she* called it – to an old woman at the tram-stop.

'What, ducks?' the old woman said disbelievingly, 'you're Super? A little old lady like you?'

'Aye, that's right,' Super Gran assured her, listing her Super-powers on her fingers. 'I've got Super-strength and Super-sight and Super-hearing and I can Super-jump and . . . Oh-oh! I've just missed the tram . . . !' She shrugged. 'Oh well, I'll catch the next one. Now, where was I . . . ?'

'You were Super-jumping!' the woman reminded her, but still not believing her.

'Oh aye. And I can Super-swim and lift heavy men and run fast and . . .'

'Well, if you can run fast,' the old woman challenged her, 'why don't you run and catch that tram . . . ?'

'Tram? But it passed ages ago,' Super Gran said, puzzled.

'Yes, ducks, the first one did. But that's the second one gone, too!' the old woman said, pointing.

Super Gran had been so engrossed in listing all her various Super-powers that she hadn't noticed that another tramcar had come – and gone!

'Oh well,' she said, 'here goes! Just watch this!'

She ran along the road between the tramlines, chasing after the vehicle – much to the amazement of the old woman. And she caught up with it and threw herself aboard, much to the amazement – and annoyance! – of the conductor.

'Here! You're not supposed to do that!' he said. 'You're only supposed to board the trams at the stops!'

'Och, laddie, there are lots of things that Super Gran

does that she's not supposed to do!' she retorted with a grin.

When the tram reached the Tower she jumped off and made for the nearest taxi rank, to get a cab to take her up to the circus ground. But it broke down half-way there – and she'd to get out and push it the rest of the way! By the time she reached the circus, things were already happening – and she was nearly too late!

Mr Black had been impatient to start his experiments and had persuaded Tub to let them into the Big Top early, before Super Gran arrived.

'The circus folk'll be back from the wedding at any minute and they'll catch us if we don't get started,' he said, panicking Tub.

'D'you think so?' Tub said hesitantly.

'Yes, let's get on with it,' Mr Black urged. 'It'll be perfectly safe.'

'But shouldn't we wait for Super Gran?' Edison said. 'She should be here any minute now.'

'Oh, don't worry,' her Dad assured her, 'we'll be all right. I *know* the Hypnotizer'll work all right.'

'But are you sure, Mr Black?' Tub asked him. He had coaxed three lions from their individual cages into the large cage in the Big Top, but now he was having second thoughts about the whole thing.

'But it's not as if he's goin' right into the cage,' Willard said. He turned to Mr Black, in his wheelchair. 'You're just doin' it from out here, aren't you?'

'That's right. I'll just poke the Hypnotizer between the bars, that's all. There's no danger. We'll *all* stay out here.' He aimed the Hypnotizer through the bars of the cage as if he was taking a photograph.

'Come on!' urged Willard. 'Let's do it, then!'

He was fed up with all the chat. He wanted some action. And, just then, they got some action . . . !

Meanwhile, Mystico had been on his way to the circus for his interview. He wasn't sure if the circus people would want him *and* Margo, or just him alone. If only *he* was employed, then Margo would have to look elsewhere.

But this didn't bother Mystico, for he knew that she wanted to break away on her own, anyway, and concentrate on a solo career. He had given her a few chances to try out different things in the act – without too much success! Instead of merely standing about, looking pretty and glamorous and handing him his various props, she had been allowed to have a go at entertaining the audience. But, apart from almost shattering their eardrums with her singing, she had tap-danced too near the edge of the stage – and had fallen into the drummer's lap! The trouble with Margo was – as an assistant she was pretty, but as an entertainer she was pretty . . . awful!

Mystico was puzzled to find that the circus was deserted. He tried everywhere. He looked in at the box-office of the Big Top – *before* Tub and the others arrived – but it was closed up. He looked in at the main office, but it too was locked up and empty. He went round all the caravans which surrounded the Big Top and the animals' cages, knocking on all the doors – but no one answered. It was all very mysterious.

'Everyone's disappeared!' he murmured, on finding not one living soul in the whole place. 'It's the Marie Celeste of the circus world!'

He didn't know, of course, that everyone – apart from Tub – was attending the wedding. And Mr Mann, the manager, had forgotten to cancel his appointment.

He wandered back to the Big Top to have a rest in one of the audience seats and to puzzle out where everyone had gone, leaving the animals behind. But, with all his rushing around, not to mention his employment worries, he fell asleep sitting in a dark corner.

He awoke, a few minutes later, to find a fat teenager, a man in a wheelchair and Willard and Edison, Super Gran's friends, clustered together outside the lions' cage, looking in at three growling lions. And the man, he saw, was poking a sort of camera thing between the bars, was explaining to the teenager how it worked – and was speaking into it! Speaking into a camera . . . ?

Mystico's first impulse was to leave his seat and go and ask them if *they* knew what was going on here at the deserted circus. But something told him to say nothing, to stay where he was – and watch. And what he saw amazed him!

'Are you *sure* it'll work, Dad?' Edison asked doubtfully.

'Of *course* it'll work. *All* my inventions work!' he told her indignantly.

'Humph!' she muttered. 'That sounds a bit like Super

60

Gran saying: "I can do *any*thing!" That's the trouble with you modest folk!'

'Yeah,' Willard agreed, 'the inventions work – until somethin' goes wrong with them!'

Mr Black ignored the insults, pointed the Hypnotizer at the restless lions inside the cage and spoke into the microphone. He told the growling, prowling animals to do as he said, then he instructed them to sit down quietly – which they did! Then he told them to stand up, to climb on the tubs they balanced on – during their act – to step down again, to sit, and then lie down. And they did everything they were told!

'Wow! Cr-rumbs!' breathed Willard, impressed.

'Yeah, not bad,' Tub agreed. 'That's quicker than Tamo, the lion tamer, can do it. And he needs a whip and a chair! That's some machine!'

'Isn't it just?' said Mr Black. 'I *knew* it would work. *All* my inventions work – didn't I tell you? So let's try it at a closer range. Let's go inside the cage and try it from there . . . !'

'What?' Edison exploded. 'You're mad, Dad!'

'Yeah,' Willard beamed, eagerly. 'Yeah, let's go inside . . . !'

'We-ell, I dunno about that . . .' Tub said hesitantly. It was one thing to try the Hypnotizer from *out*side the cage, there was no danger in that. But from *in*side . . . ? That was another matter.

Mr Black and Willard took sides against Edison and Tub at first. But Tub soon gave in when Mr Black reminded him that he'd had lessons from the lion tamer and said he was sure that Tub would cope all right. Then he flattered him about his Super-strength, but kidded him on that it was all fat!

'It's not fat!' Tub denied. 'It's muscles! Super-muscles . . . !'

'And besides,' Mr Black went on, 'what could possibly go wrong? You've seen the Hypnotizer working, haven't you? You *know* it hypnotizes the lions . . .'

'Yeah . . . yeah, that's right,' Tub agreed. 'I forgot about that.'

So this meant it was now three to one against stick-in-the-mud Edison. And the three got their way. Despite the fact that she tried to persuade them to wait until Super Gran arrived, just in case.

'But what can go *wrong*?' her Dad asked her. 'See, I'll control them from out here, first. I'll put them under the influence – and *then* we'll go in. There'll be no danger whatsoever.'

'Oh well, if you're sure . . .' she said reluctantly, as Tub opened the cage and they all trooped inside.

To begin with, everything went all right. But then:

'Oops! Butter-fingers . . . !' cried Mr Black as the Hypnotizer slipped out of his hands.

Before anyone could catch it, it hit the ground and the 'stop' button accidentally got pressed – switching the machine off! The lions – no longer hypnotized – suddenly ferociously turned to face Mr Black, Edison, Willard and Tub.

'Oh-oh! I've done it now!' said Mr Black.

Trapped in a cage with three angry lions, Edison

screamed and ran in panic. But she ran the wrong way! Instead of staying beside the others, she ran in the opposite direction – and one of the lions went after her!

Tub, without Tamo's chair and whip, faced up to the second lion and yelled his battle-cry '*Aieeeee* ...' at it, daring it to attack him. While the third lion padded softly, but threateningly, towards Mr Black and Willard.

'Yeeks!' yelled Willard.

Mystico, sitting quietly and unobserved in his dark corner seat, had seen all this. But he was rooted to the spot in terror, unable to think of a way to save them.

However, he didn't have long to think about it, for help was at hand in the frail, unlikely, elderly shape of – Super Gran!

She had walked through the circus gateway in time to hear the scream from Edison, the shouts from Willard, Tub and Mr Black – and the roars of the lions. She dashed into the Big Top. 'What's wrong ...? Oh-oh ...!'

At a glance she took in what was happening and she raced towards the cage: 'Look out ...! Stand back ...!'

Inside the cage, Super Gran, unexpectedly, did *not* run towards the lion on the left that was threatening Edison, nor to the one on the right threatening Mr Black and Willard. Instead she dashed between the two of them – and grabbed each one by its tail, holding both of them back at once from attacking her friends.

'Here puss, puss!' she teased.

The two lions, yelping with rage – and astonishment! – at this, turned to face her, roaring angrily. But Super Gran merely ran away from them, forward, towards the

back of the cage, still holding on to their tails, taking the lions with her. And this had the effect of making them twist round, surprised, so that they were now facing the *front* of the cage.

Then, before they could recover, Super Gran ran back again – backwards! – towards the *front* of the cage, forcing the astonished lions to whip round until they were staring at the *back* of the cage! And she did the same thing again, and again, until the poor, confused lions were utterly exhausted – and sat down on the ground, refusing to *move*, let alone attack anyone! – sorry, by now, that they'd started the whole thing in the first place!

'There! That's fixed *them*!' she said, dusting off her hands in triumph.

'Thanks, Super Gran,' said Edison, cowering in a corner.

'Wow, did you see that?' exclaimed Willard proudly.

Meanwhile, Tub had been wrestling with the third lion. But now, with the little amount of training he'd had from the lion tamer – plus his Super-strength – he had persuaded the lion to join its two tired friends for a rest on the ground!

'Come on, let's get out,' said Mr Black, as he steered his chair to the exit.

Willard and Edison joined him in escaping from the cage, with Willard picking up the dropped Hypnotizer on the way. Then they were followed by Super Gran and Tub, who closed and locked the cage behind him.

Once they were all safely outside the cage, Mr Black tried out the Hypnotizer again to check that its fall hadn't damaged it. It hadn't. He hypnotized the lions and then, satisfied that the machine was working properly, he reversed the sound-beam to leave the lions the way they had found them, un-hypnotized – but now decidedly dazed!

'Well, the Hypnotizer worked all right, didn't it!' Mr Black said calmly.

'Yes,' Edison agreed, shaking nervously with fright, 'until it fell!'

'Oh well, accidents'll happen!' he grinned. 'Don't worry about it.' He swung his chair round until he was facing Super Gran. '*I've* got to go back to Chisleton now. But I'll leave the Hypnotizer with *you*, for you to experiment with on your travels round the country, okay?'

'Well – aye – okay, if you insist,' she replied, slightly puzzled. She wasn't quite sure who – or what – he intended her to experiment *on*!

Then, after saying cheerio to Tub, they all left the Big Top: Super Gran and the children to return to Muttlin's, and Mr Black to head for the railway station and home.

Mystico, meanwhile, unnoticed by Super Gran and company – who'd had other more important things on their minds! – had been pressing himself down into the seat, in the shadows, a thoughtful look on his face. He had seen what happened when Mr Black operated the Hypnotizer, how the lions were completely under its control – and he was impressed.

Suddenly – he had the answers to all his problems! He realized how his dream, his ambition, could become a reality.

The answer was – the Hypnotizer! For not only could it be an additional gimmick for his great new stage act – it would also be the means of getting Super Gran to work for him. And all he'd have to do was – hypnotize her!

If he could just get hold of it somehow, he'd be able to make her work for him. He resolved to steal it if need be.

'I'll hypnotize 'er – with the Hypnotizer!' he murmured to himself with a self-satisfied smirk . . .

6 Mystico's Challenge

Mystico lounged in his seat in the Big Top, his hands clasped behind his head. He was smiling, daydreaming about the new, prosperous, glorious future which stretched ahead of him. He would have the greatest magic show in Britain – no, in the world! It would be like the magnificent ones which used to tour all over the country in his father's and his grandfather's day. It would be a complete magic show, not like the rather crummy little act he had at present.

It would be stupendous and would tour all the big cities, ending up with a special season in London. Then it would go abroad – to Europe, America, Australia, Africa, South America – everywhere! And it would have everything in it – acrobats, jugglers, trapeze artists, clowns, tightrope walkers – the lot!

But the star of the show – apart from himself, of course! – would be Super Gran, hypnotized if need be! And she would show off her Super-powers on a full-time professional basis.

On the other hand, he thought, maybe he *wouldn't* exactly offer her the double salary he had promised before. He wouldn't need to, once she was hypnotized. For then she would accept whatever he offered. In fact, he wouldn't even have to pay her the *original* salary he had thought of. Or better still – why pay her at *all*? If he was going to hypnotize her he'd be able to get her to work for him for nothing – just by suggesting it to her!

But first things first. And the first thing was to get hold of the machine. That was his immediate problem. How was he going to do it?

'M'mm, let's see,' he muttered. 'Edison's Dad's going to Chisleton – wherever *that* is – so that's *him* out the way. And the fat youth works here in the circus, so he'll be too busy. So that just leaves Super Gran and those kids.'

He got up out of his seat. 'But how am I going to get it? I'll have to have a good old think about this.'

But the thought of actually getting his hands on the Hypnotizer was enough to make him do a little jig all the way out of the Big Top.

'Tee, hee, hee!' he chortled. 'I'm going to hypnotize 'er – with the Hypnotizer . . . !'

As he left the tent a car came screaming in through the circus gateway and screeched to a halt in front of him. Then a man popped his head out of the driver's window.

'Ah! Mr Mystico?' he asked. 'Looking for the manager, Mr Mann?'

Mystico nodded.

'Then *I'm* your man. *I* put the Mann in *man*ager!' He laughed. 'Must apologize and all that. We were all at a wedding when I suddenly remembered, halfway through the reception, about our appointment. So sorry!'

'Yes . . . I . . . I've been waiting in the . . . ah . . . Big Top . . .' Mystico said.

But Mr Mann was more concerned with the speech

he'd just made at the wedding than with Mystico's interview. 'I must tell you the jokes I cracked at the reception, I really must. Good, they were. Listen . . .'

'Yes . . . but . . . you see . . . I . . .' Mystico began, but Mr Mann wouldn't listen. He absolutely *insisted* on telling his jokes.

'It was our bearded lady who was getting married, to our india-rubber man, you see? And I cracked this joke . . .' He paused. 'You'll like it . . .'

'Not a lot . . . !' muttered Mystico.

'*I* said,' said Mr Mann, 'that the bride – the bearded lady, remember? – was previously engaged – to a barber! But she got out of the engagement. Boy, was that a *close shave*!'

He exploded with laughter at his joke and then, before Mystico could reply – or escape! – he continued: 'And the groom – the india-rubber man, remember? Oh, by the way, he used to play in a band – a rubber band!' He laughed again. 'Well anyway, he was up in court recently on a parking offence. And the judge threatened to give him a long stretch! A long stretch, get it?' He chortled cheerily. 'And then I said . . .'

'Look, er . . . Mr Mann . . . I . . . I don't really . . . ah . . . need the job here after all. Something else has turned up,' said Mystico.

He *nearly* added: 'Something a lot better than your little circus. Something stupendous, gigantic, majestic – my very own grand, lavish, magical stage show. The one I have always wanted, always yearned for. It's within my grasp.'

'What? You don't want the job?' Mr Mann looked puzzled for a moment.

But then he thought of the wedding reception which was still going on without him. And he thought of some more jokes he could crack, if he could just get back there in time. So he put his car into gear, said cheerio and shot out through the gateway at speed, the way he'd come in.

As he drove he muttered to himself, rehearsing his new jokes: 'The groom used to work in a disco – as a bouncer! India-rubber man – bouncer! Ha, ha! And the bride put somebody out of her house and said: "A moustache" – "a moustache you to leave"! Ho, ho, ho . . .!'

Mystico, in turn, climbed into his vehicle and slowly followed the manager's car out through the gateway. As he went he murmured to himself: 'I'm going to hypnotize 'er – with the Hypnotizer . . .!' He glanced to his left, towards the park, and then he got the germ of an idea, an idea which might just solve his problem – the problem of how he was going to get hold of the Hypnotizer.

When Mystico came off the stage after his first performance that evening, he hung around in the wings to watch Super Gran, while Margo hurried back to their dressing-room. And it was there, in the wings, that Mystico got another couple of ideas. He got the first one while listening to Super Gran boasting! And he got the second one when he saw Willard and Edison using their CB radios to communicate in the wings, from one side of the stage to the other, while Super Gran performed.

'I can do *anything*!' Super Gran boasted, making her

usual claim, as the audience yelled for her to do bigger and better tricks.

'Could you push a Slackpool tram along its tramlines?' a man yelled.

'Aye, laddie. No bother at all!' she replied.

'Could you push a train?' asked a woman, laughing.

'Easy-peasy!'

'Could you climb Slackpool Tower?' asked a little boy.

'I told you, sonny – I can do *anything* . . . !'

Mystico stepped forward out of the wings, on to the stage. 'Very well, Super Gran, *I* – Mystico the Magician – challenge you. To a race – to the top of the tower!'

He twirled his cloak in his usual theatrical gesture – successfully this time, he'd been practising! – and he touched his top hat to her in a salute, then bowed an exaggerated bow. 'A race – to the *very* top of the Tower!'

'What? You?' Super Gran was taken aback.

'And I'm so confident of winning,' Mystico added, 'that I'll put a little wager on with you!'

'Och laddie, I don't bet.'

'Not even on a *sure* thing?' he asked, as he stroked his beard.

'There's no such thing as a *sure* thing,' Super Gran pointed out.

'Are you *sure*?'

'*Sure*, I'm *sure*!'

Mystico laughed. 'But *surely* there is? The *sure* thing that Super Gran can climb Slackpool tower faster than Mystico?' he teased. 'I may be mistaken, but I thought you just said that you could do *anything*?'

'I did. And I can. *Anything*!'

'*Can* you?' Mystico challenged, with a smirk. 'If you're so sure of yourself, put it to the test. I'll bet you £100 … no, £200 … no, I'll tell you what – I'll bet you a month's salary I can beat you to the top of the tower.'

'Right, you're on!' Super Gran agreed. Not that she *wanted* Mystico's money, but she could always give it to charity.

'But what stake are *you* putting up?' Mystico asked. 'For *me* to collect, when *I* win the race? M'mm?'

'What's he talkin' about a steak for?' Willard asked Edison over the CB radio from his side of the stage to her side. 'Is it a steak and chips?'

'No, silly,' Edison retorted. 'It's not *that* kind of steak! And against Super Gran – he's *had* his chips!' She laughed. 'No, it's the S.T.A.K.E. kind of stake,' she said, spelling it out for him. 'The money you put on for a bet.'

On stage, Super Gran turned to Mystico: 'And what stake do *you* suggest I put up?'

She reckoned it didn't matter *what* he suggested, there was no way he was going to win it anyway. Not against *her*. Not against Super Gran – that was impossible!

'The Hypnotizer!' Mystico replied without hesitation. 'That's what I want *you* to put up.'

'What? The Hypnotizer? But what do *you* know about the Hypnotizer?'

He gestured towards the restive audience, who wanted Super Gran to get on with her performance and stop chatting with Mystico the Magician.

'You'd better continue with your demonstration.

73

We'll discuss the details later. But remember – you *have* accepted my challenge. And in public too. In front of the audience.' He gestured towards them.

Afterwards, when Super Gran had left the stage, Mystico explained to her and the children how he'd come to be in the Big Top and had seen the Hypnotizer in action. Edison drew Super Gran to one side.

'But you can't put up the Hypnotizer as a stake. It's not yours – it's *Dad's*!'

'Och, havers, lassie. What're you worrying about? There's no way that a scunner like yon is going to beat *me* to the top of Slackpool Tower, is there?'

'Super Gran – what *is* a scunner ...?' Edison asked, not for the first time!

But Super Gran was so amazed at Mystico even suggesting such a thing – and so amazed at Edison for thinking that she – Super Gran! – could possibly *lose* the bet – that she didn't hear Edison's question, as usual!

'Don't worry,' she assured the girl in a whisper, as they returned to Mystico and Willard, 'the Hypnotizer is safe! Believe me!'

'Oh,' said Mystico, 'and there's another suggestion I'd like to make. There may be a crowd of people watching our race – after all, I'm sure your audience will come along, just to see if you win or not ...!'

'Win? Of course I'll win, laddie!' Super Gran insisted confidently. 'I told you – I can do ...'

'*Anything*! Yes, I know,' Mystico interrupted. 'But anyway, in case there's a crowd, we don't want to lose touch with each other – so I suggest we each use one of those walkie-talkie things the children have. To keep in contact with one another. Yes?'

'Aye, okay, laddie,' Super Gran agreed cheerfully, humouring the man. 'Whatever you say. Though I don't know why you're bothering!'

'And shall we say – three o'clock for the race to start? Agreed?'

Super Gran nodded. 'Aye, whatever you say is all right by me, son.'

Mystico couldn't wait to get away from Super Gran and company – to get rubbing his hands together in glee! By tomorrow, just after three o'clock – the Hypnotizer would be his!

'I'm going to hypnotize 'er – with the Hypnotizer!' he sang joyfully to himself as he danced merrily along the corridor to the dressing-room.

When he and Margo went back on stage that evening, for the second house, both their minds were on things other than their act. Mystico had told Margo about the Hypnotizer, of how it was going to save their careers and was going to lead eventually – once he'd hypnotized Super Gran – to Mystico's very own super-duper magical touring show.

But Margo wasn't too interested in hearing about what the Hypnotizer could do. She was busily dreaming her own daydreams, of her glittering show-biz career, of going to America to be a big film star . . .

As they did their 'mind-reading' act, Mystico cringed every time he asked Margo to identify an object which he'd taken from the audience. For, not only was she getting the secret codes mixed up as usual, but, as she was thinking constantly about her film career, her answers were even *sillier* than usual!

When he asked her: 'What do I *have here*? What am I *holding*?' – which was the code for 'a lady's gold bracelet' – she replied: 'Hollywood'!

As the audience fell about laughing at Margo's reply Mystico gnashed his teeth. But he consoled himself with the thought that once he'd got hold of the Hypnotizer his troubles – including Margo – would be over. Hollywood was welcome to her!

Then an idea for reviving the act struck him. As the audience was falling about with laughter, they might as well capitalize on it. If it was laughing anyway, *at* her, it might as well laugh at her *jokes*! So he decided to give her a chance to tell some, to help boost her solo career. After all, she'd tried just about everything else! So he whispered a reminder about Mr Mann's jokes, which he'd told her just before the show started.

'The bearded lady . . .' he whispered out of the side of his mouth. 'And the india-rubber man . . .'

'What? Bearded what?' said Margo in a loud voice. 'Oh . . . oh yes . . . let me see now, how did it go . . . ?'

While the audience continued to laugh at her, Margo took the opportunity to go through the joke, mouthing it silently, practising it before she dared to say it out loud. Then:

'Oh yes . . . ahem . . .' She cleared her throat. 'There was this bride – who was the bearded lady in the circus. And she was engaged previously – to a barber, but she got out of it . . .' She paused, before delivering the punch-line – then delivered the wrong one! 'And boy, did she get her hair cut short . . . no, that wasn't right, was it?' She turned for guidance to Mystico, who cringed again. 'No, she got a close shave, didn't she? But wait a minute, brides don't shav – oh, I see! She was the *bearded* lady, wasn't she . . . oh yes, very good . . .'

Mystico, realizing he'd made a mistake in letting Margo loose on the audience, tried to haul her back and get her off the stage. But Margo had got into her stride and was determined to keep going.

'And did you hear the one about the india-rubber man?' she went on. 'Well, he was in court and the judge said . . . er . . . um . . . what did he say, Mystico?' She turned and appealed to her boss, but Mystico's face merely flushed with embarrassment, and he shrugged. The audience roared with laughter.

'Oh yes . . .' she remembered – or thought she did! 'The judge said he was going to get rubber banned . . . was that it? No, wasn't it something to do with a stretch, or something . . . ?'

Mystico, groaning, this time succeeded in hauling Margo off the stage into the wings. He hoped that the audience hadn't noticed just how bad she was, but reckoned that that was too much to hope for!

He silently prayed that he'd get hold of the Hypnotizer the next day, as planned – before Margo ruined their act altogether!

7 Tower Power!

'Where's Magic Ian?' Willard asked, looking at the crowds.

It was three o'clock the next day, and Super Gran, Willard and Edison were standing at the foot of Slackpool Tower, near the front entrance on the promenade. They had been seeking Mystico for the last ten minutes, but there was no sign of him.

'That's his battered old van over there,' Willard went on, pointing to where it stood across the road, at the kerb on the sea side of the prom, near the pier. 'So he must be about here somewhere.'

'Yes, but where?' said Super Gran, looking around.

Edison grabbed Super Gran's arm and pushed her cardigan sleeve up to look at her watch. 'He's late, Super Gran. It's almost five past. You go ahead and start climbing.'

'Maybe he's gone to another entrance?' Super Gran said as they continued to scan the passing crowds for the missing Mystico. 'We'll give him a few more minutes, eh?'

'No, Super Gran, I don't think we should. *He* said to start at three o'clock – so if *he's* late, then that's hard luck on *him*!'

This was rather harsh, coming from Edison. But she

was annoyed at Mystico betting against the Hypnotizer, and if he lost the race through being late then that was *his* lookout and no one else's.

Suddenly, before anyone could say anything else, Mystico's voice came crackling through on Willard's CB radio, which Super Gran was wearing, strapped around her neck, in its box.

'Hello, are you there, Super Gran? This is Mystico the Magician here. What's keeping you? I'm a quarter of the way up the tower already!'

'What? A quarter way up?' Super Gran exclaimed, taken aback. She reckoned that he must have entered by another entrance, but didn't take time to ask him.

She dived inside the building, followed by the others, and took the lift up as far as it went, to a floor where there was a restaurant, a ballroom and a disco. Then they took a second lift to a floor with an amusements centre, full of Space Invaders, TV computer games and pinball machines. Next they took the 'rocket' express lift the rest of the way up the Tower, as far as the public could go, to the viewing platform.

And all the way up in these various lifts Mystico's voice kept coming crackling through to them on the CB radio, giving a running commentary: 'I've reached the half-way stage ... I'm almost three-quarters-way there now ... I don't see any sign of *you* ... you *are* racing me, aren't you? I've passed the three-quarters mark ... I'm almost there ...'

When Super Gran and company reached this top viewing platform they realized that the general public weren't allowed to go any higher. After that there was only a narrow ladder – for Tower repair-men and electricians – fastened to the bare framework, going right up to the very top, to a tiny platform. And the public – definitely! – were not allowed on this ladder.

But that, of course, didn't stop Super Gran! If it was a race to the top of the Tower, then it was a race to the *very* top of the Tower! She glanced round, saw there was no one watching, gave her handbag – which contained the Hypnotizer – to Edison for safe-keeping, and clambered over the railing.

'Oh, Super Gran,' Edison said, alarmed, 'do you think you should?'

'Of course, lassie, how else can I climb to the top? This is the only way!'

'Yeah, go to it, Gran!' Willard encouraged her.

She put her foot on the narrow ladder and began climbing, but Edison was *really* beginning to have second thoughts.

'Super Gran, come down! It looks awful dangerous! You're not *supposed* to go up there!'

'Wheesht, lassie! Not so loud or someone'll hear you and come and stop me!'

As she climbed the ladder she could still hear Mystico's voice coming from the radio, from its box around her neck, telling her that he had reached the top – but where was *she*? What was keeping her?

Imagine her astonishment, therefore, when she reached the very topmost platform – hardly big enough to stand on! – to find that she had the place to herself! There was absolutely no sign of Mystico. That is, not unless he was the Invisible Man!

'Where *is* that scunnery Magic Ian?' she muttered.

She took a look round, admiring the view far below her of the piers and the coastline from Sleetwood in the north to St Dan's in the south, then she quickly climbed back down the ladder – sliding most of the way! She hoped to reach the viewing platform, where Willard and Edison – with Edison on edge! – were patiently waiting for her, before a Tower official caught her and she got into trouble for trespassing.

She made it, safely, and wasn't caught. Edison breathed a sigh of relief. But Super Gran *still* couldn't understand where Mystico had got to.

'Do you think he's still on the ground, just pretending he's climbed it?' Edison asked, when Super Gran explained about her 'invisible' opponent.

'What would be the point?' Super Gran said. 'He must know I'd climb right to the top and discover he wasn't there. And where was he speaking *from*?'

Before they could discuss the mystery any further, Mystico's voice crackled through on the radio again: 'Oh, by the way, Super Gran – in case you don't believe I reached the top of the tower I've got a witness here . . . who climbed it with me!'

'What? *Two* of them?' Super Gran exclaimed. 'Jings! I didn't even see *one* of them, never mind *two*! *Two* Invisible Men!'

'And he's prepared to swear, in case there's an argument,' Mystico continued, 'that I climbed it. He's Mr Nelson and he's a taxi driver. Mr Nelson . . .'

The man came on the air. 'Breaker, breaker. Do you read me?' He kidded himself that he knew a bit of CB jargon – but not a lot! 'Hello folks, my name's Nelson and I'm the taxi driver who brought Mr Mystico up here . . .'

'Up *here*? Up the *Tower*?' said Edison, mystified. 'But how *could* he?' She looked around the viewing platform on the extremely remote chance that there was a taxi there somewhere!

'Yes,' Mr Nelson went on, 'up here – to Scanley Park . . .'

'Scanley Park?' Super Gran and company stared at each other blankly.

'And I'm bringing him back down to the prom straight away to collect his winnings. Roger, over and out, good buddies . . . !'

'Scanley Park?' said Super Gran, puzzled. 'What's Magic Ian doing up there?'

Edison suddenly snapped her fingers. 'That's it . . . !'

'*What's* it?' asked Willard.

'Scanley Park . . .'

'Yes, they *said* that,' agreed Super Gran patiently. 'So what?'

'Don't you see? Don't you remember?' said Edison. 'We played with the frisbee at Scanley Park the other day, and you threw it at that little building near the tennis courts? That little *tower* . . . that titchy, *little* stone *tower*! So *that's* what Magic Ian climbed while you were wasting your time climbing the *real* Slackpool Tower!' She was extremely mad, as indeed they all were.

While they were on their way down from the viewing platform and while Mystico was on his way back from Scanley Park in the taxi, they – Super Gran and Mystico – argued about it over their CB radios. Mystico claimed that he hadn't actually said it was to be the *large* Slackpool Tower, the one on the prom, that they were to race up – just Slackpool tower. *Any* Slackpool tower! And it wasn't *his* fault if she had chosen to climb the higher – the *much* higher! – of the two! Nobody, after all, had *made* her climb that big one on the prom!

'But of course,' he went on, 'if you're not prepared to honour your bet, then that's all right by me. But what will the Muttlin's audiences say when I tell them about it – at every performance from now on . . .?'

'But you were cheated, Gran,' Willard said, when Super Gran told them she'd have to stick to her bargain and hand over the Hypnotizer.

'Aye, laddie, I was. But that can't be helped. It's my own fault for making the bet in the first place.'

'But that means,' said Edison, 'you'll have to hand over the Hypnotizer – *Dad's* Hypnotizer! – after being cheated out of it.'

Super Gran shrugged. 'That's it, Edison. I made a bet with yon scunnery Magic Ian and I've got to pay up. You've got to honour your bets.'

She was furious; more with herself than with Mystico. She was angry at having been conned out of the Hypnotizer, of course, but she was even angrier at herself for accepting the bet in the first place. She had only done so because she'd been sure of winning. The remote possibility of losing had never crossed her mind. But she'd never expected Mystico to cheat her, either.

Super Gran and company came back down to earth again from the dizzy heights of the Tower, by means of the various lifts, and reached ground level at the prom. Super Gran lifted the Hypnotizer out of her handbag and looked at it.

'Och well, lassie, don't worry! Your Dad'll be able to make another one without too much bother, won't he?'

Edison shrugged. 'I suppose so. It's just the idea of being cheated out of it, that's all.'

'Aye, but apart from that, there's no harm done, is there? It's not as if Magic Ian's going to hypnotize anyone with it. He's probably just going to use it in his act, that's all . . .' Little did she know!

A few minutes later a taxi came whizzing round the corner and stopped at the Tower entrance. Mystico jumped out, paid Mr Nelson and approached the downcast trio jauntily and confidently. He was wearing his full stage gear – top hat, cloak, black suit, moustache and beard – in public, in broad daylight! No wonder everyone turned to stare at him!

Willard pointed to his van, still parked across the street and now being closely inspected by a woman traffic warden, her notebook at the ready.

'Isn't that your van over there?' he asked.

Mystico nodded without even looking at it. 'Yes, I

parked it there and took a taxi to the park. It's quicker than my clapped-out chariot. And besides, I needed a witness, didn't I? Ah! Is that the Hypnotizer, all ready for me? Then I'll take it. Thank you ...!' As he took it from Super Gran, he gloated.

'We wondered what you wanted it for,' Super Gran said, 'and *I* said it was probably to use in your act. Is that right?'

'In my act? Well ... eh ... um ... er ... yes, yes that's right. For the act. On stage. Me and Margo ...' He was caught unawares. He obviously couldn't tell her what he *really* wanted it for – to hypnotize *her* to make her join the act which, eventually, would lead to his super-duper stage show. So he quickly had to think up some convincing lies.

'Ah ... er ... Margo and I have a ... um ... sort of hypnotism act, but I thought that if I ... er ... used the ... um ... Hypnotizer it would improve it a lot. I'll *really* be able to hypnotize her now, instead of just pretending to. See?'

Super Gran saw, all right! For she'd tuned in her mind-reading powers and caught his earlier thoughts – the ones about using the Hypnotizer on *her* and making her join his act against her will.

So she'd have to be careful to keep out of his way as much as possible, she thought, so that he couldn't use it on her. And the most likely time for him to use it was while she was on stage, for she'd be at her most vulnerable there. But luckily she had only that evening's performances to worry about, for this was her last day at Slackpool and she'd be safe, she thought, when they moved on to Tornmouth.

But suddenly she realized that Mystico intended using it on her – there and then! He lifted it up, looked intently at it and held it near his face. And with only the slightest effort he'd be able to press the button, shout a command into the microphone – and hypnotize her!

'How does it work?' he asked innocently. 'Do I just point it at someone and speak in here ...?' He was quickly reading the instructions which Mr Black – thoughtfully! – had written out and attached to one of its sides.

But Super Gran read his mind – as quickly as *he* read the instructions!

'Aye, something like that!' she said as she edged away from him and tried to signal to Willard and Edison, with nods and grimaces, to make a quick getaway.

But they didn't catch on! They just stood staring at her and wondered why she was making funny faces at them! Then she remembered that Mystico still had Edison's CB radio transceiver.

'Oh, by the way – the lassie'll have her radio back, if you don't mind!' she said. 'That wasn't part of your winnings!'

Mystico looked up from studying the instructions. 'Oh yes, I'd forgotten about that in the excitement – of collecting the Hypnotizer, you know!' He pulled the radio from his pocket and gave it to Edison. 'Here you are ...'

While Mystico's attention was on *Edison* and was off

her, Super Gran suddenly pushed the children into the passing crowd, milling about the Tower entrance.

'Run, kids . . . !' she yelled.

'Huh?' Willard and Edison were both taken aback – as was Mystico! – by the sudden command, but they knew Super Gran well enough by now to run, without questioning it, when she told them to. So they ran! And *she* ran with them!

'Here! Wait a minute, I'm not ready . . . !' complained Mystico. 'Curses!'

He'd been caught unawares while trying to aim the Hypnotizer at Super Gran who, desperately trying to evade the machine's hypnotizing rays, was diving into the crowd to disappear.

Mystico, looking round for something to stand on, jumped up on a concrete waste-paper bin. This gave him the height needed to see over the heads of the crowd and he located Super Gran as she ran, weaved and dodged amongst them.

Taking extra-careful aim at her running figure, he pressed the various buttons. Getting the correct sequence of lights but not having time to think of the exact instructions he wanted to give her, he said, on the spur of the moment, the first command that came into his head: 'You'll do what I tell you – the next time I speak to you!'

And *that*, he thought, should do the trick. Super Gran would be under his control – any second now!

8 Margo's Memory

As Super Gran rushed into the crowd to escape, she
decided to try an experiment with one of her Super-
powers. She had never tried this before and didn't know
if it would work or not. But she was desperate, and
willing to try anything to 'prevent herself being
hypnotized by Mystico.

She knew that he would be aiming the Hypnotizer
at her from the back, and she knew that she could
duck down to dodge the ray as it shot out. But she
couldn't run in a crouched position for long, as he
would see her doing it and would lower his aim accord-
ingly.

But, on the other hand, if she could duck down
immediately before he pressed the button – *then* she could
dodge the ray just as it left the machine, and it would
miss her.

She didn't want to look round at him or he'd suspect
what she had in mind. So she sent out a 'beam' of mind-
reading power backwards towards Mystico and, sure
enough, just as he pressed the 'on' button she picked up
the message from his mind that he was doing so. She
ducked – at exactly the right moment – and the ray
shot out silently and passed harmlessly over her head.
And by the time the magician realized he'd missed her

and pressed the button again, Super Gran had escaped into a shop doorway.

But although the hypnotizing ray missed Super Gran – it hit someone else; someone who was standing across the road from the Tower, inspecting a certain rusting vehicular heap and noting details of it in her notebook. But Mystico didn't discover this until a few minutes later.

'Curses! I missed her!' he groaned. 'But how did she manage to duck just as I fired at her? Humph! She's got *all* the luck!'

Not that it *was* luck, of course, but Mystico didn't know that.

'Well, that's it,' he muttered. 'I've lost her in the crowd. I'll just have to try again later. *I* know! I'll do it when she's on stage tonight – from the wings. She'll be defenceless there! That's the very thing . . . !'

He crossed the prom to his van, where the traffic warden was still hanging about.

'Is this your van, sir?' she asked politely. He nodded. 'Then I'm afraid it's parked illegally. I'll have to give you a parking ticket . . .' She got out her ticket-pad.

'Oh, go and jump off the pier!' Mystico muttered in annoyance – then stared, open-mouthed, as the woman obeyed his command!

She ran to the pier near by, threw her admission money into the pay-box, pushed her way through the turnstile, dashed along the length of the pier – and jumped off it into the sea below!

'Here! I heard that!' a stout woman passerby said angrily to Mystico. 'You told that there meter-maid to jump off the pier!' The woman, like Mystico, had been standing, dumb-founded by this performance, but had now regained her voice. 'Here! You'd better do something about it!'

'Me? Why me?' asked Mystico.

'Cos you *told* her to do it, that's why! And she *did* it, that's why! And I *heard* you, that's why!' She turned to other passersby and pointed at Mystico. 'He *told* her to do it, he did . . . !'

'Oh, all right, all right!' said Mystico. 'Don't go on so.'

He ran to the pay-box, threw his coins in, pushed through the turnstile, ran along the pier and jumped off into the water – before he remembered . . .

'He-elp . . . ! I can't swim . . . glug . . . !'

But help was at hand.

'Don't worry – *I'll* save you . . . !' said a woman in uniform who – luckily for Mystico – was swimming around rather competently near by.

It was the woman traffic warden – the meter-maid! The shock of hitting the water had cancelled the effect of the Hypnotizer!

'Although what *I'm* doing in here,' she said, 'I'll never know. How *did* I get here, do *you* know? Hey! Aren't you that van-owner?' She reached for her pen and ticket-pad which were floating near by. Once a traffic warden, always a traffic warden! 'Now, let's see – your van number is . . . ?'

'Glug, glug, glug . . . !' said Mystico.

*

That evening at Muttlin's theatre, Super Gran was rather uneasy as she performed her act, for she knew she'd be at Mystico's mercy. All *he* had to do was stand in the wings, aim the Hypnotizer at her and – bingo! – she'd be hypnotized. So she got Willard and Edison to stand in the wings – one each side of the stage – during her performance, as a precaution.

Mystico, coming along to the stage with the Hypnotizer in his pocket, saw the children there, realized that he couldn't do anything in public, in front of witnesses, and withdrew again to bide his time. For he thought he had plenty of time to do this. He didn't know that Super Gran's two weeks at the Slackpool Muttlin's were coming to an end that night.

'What?' he stormed, when Margo told him, the next day. 'She's gone? Gone where? What do you mean?'

'I told you before,' Margo pouted, 'but you didn't listen to me. You *never* listen to me . . .'

'Never mind all that. Just tell me again – where's she gone?'

'She's moved on to another Muttlin's Centre some-where . . .'

'Yes, but where? Which one? There's a dozen Muttlin's Centres. Which one has *she* gone to? I thought you said she told you?'

'She did. But I've forgotten,' admitted Margo.

'Forgotten!' Mystico stamped around their dressing-room angrily. He threw chairs over, banged their make-up jars about on the dressing-table and opened the door

– just so that he could slam it shut again! 'Forgotten? Forgotten?'

'We-ell …' Margo giggled. 'You know what my memory's like. It's not all *that* great. You know that I can't remem –'

'Memory?' Mystico interrupted. 'Memory! I wonder …?'

'Wonder? Wonder what?'

'I wonder if perhaps the Hypnotizer could aid your memory, m'mm?'

'What? The Hypnotizer? What do you mean?'

'I mean,' Mystico smirked, 'if I used the Hypnotizer on you, and …'

'On *me*? The Hypnotizer? No way! It might be dangerous. It *will* be dangerous. Oh no, you're not trying it out on me …!'

But while Margo was protesting, Mystico was secretly slipping it out of his pocket and switching it on behind his back. And now, before the girl realized what was happening, he suddenly pointed it at her.

'You'll do as I say … What will you do …?' he said.

'I'll do as you say …' Margo replied dreamily.

It worked.

'Now to try it out on her memory,' Mystico muttered. 'Will it work on *that*? It'll be a miracle if it does! But, on the other hand, everything she's ever seen, heard and learned is in there somewhere – amongst all the clutter! All I've got to do is draw it out.'

But the Hypnotizer worked perfectly and the information was easily extracted.

'Tell me – where is Super Gran going next, on her tour of the Muttlin's Holiday Centres?' he asked.

'She's going down to Tornmouth,' Margo replied dreamily.

'And where else is she going on her tour?' he continued. He might as well get *all* the information while he was at it, he thought. It would save time and trouble later on.

'She's going along the coast to Beastbourne, then up to Tarborough to finish off,' she told him, talking rather like a robot.

Mystico then instructed Margo to forget that she had been hypnotized, and he *un*-hypnotized her. And when she 'awoke' she remembered nothing about it!

'Right then!' he said. 'Get your things packed.'

'Why? Where are we going?'

'To Tornmouth.'

'Tornmouth? Why Tornmouth?' she asked. 'I thought we were booked in here for another couple of weeks? Why Tornmouth?'

'Because that's where Super Gran's gone, that's why.'

'How do you know?' she asked suspiciously. She knew he hadn't used the Hypnotizer on her – or at least she *thought* he hadn't! So how had he managed to find out where Super Gran was?

'Oh ... er ... ah ... I happened to remember what you told me previously. Yes, that's what it was. I ... ah ... um ... remembered ...' he lied.

But now there was a problem. If they walked out on their job here at Slackpool, could they possibly get

another one at Tornmouth? They had to live on something until Mystico hypnotized Super Gran and
managed to get his new show on the road.

Mystico thought about that for a while. Then
suddenly it dawned on him. He could use the Hypnotizer
for that, too! All he had to do was to go to Tornmouth,
walk into a variety theatre – and hypnotize the manager
into giving him a job for as long as it suited him! Once
he had Super Gran working for him and once he had
his big, new magical show, he wouldn't need to resort
to these tricks. But, in the meantime, he would have
to!

The thought flitted briefly through his mind that he
could take this hypnotizing business a stage further and
cut out work altogether! All he'd have to do was – to go
to a *bank* manager and hypnotize him into opening his
safe and handing the money over to Mystico!

But he quickly rejected this idea. In the first place
– it was dishonest! And secondly – Mystico actually *liked*
to work, he liked going on the stage and entertaining
people. Or at least, trying to!

'We're going down to Tornmouth to hypnotize Super
Gran,' he told Margo. 'And we'll hypnotize a theatre
manager while we're at it, to get a job. Just to tide us
over until we hypnotize Super Gran.'

'But what if we *don't* catch up with her in Tornmouth?'
Margo asked. 'Or you don't manage to hypnotize her?'

'We will,' Mystico replied confidently. 'But if we don't
catch up with her at Tornmouth, then we'll follow her
to the other Muttlin's Centres at Beastbourne and

97

Tarborough. In fact, we'll follow her all over Britain if necessary!'

'Hey! How did *you* know she was going to Beastbourne and Tarborough?' Margo asked suspiciously.

'I *told* you, Margo,' Mystico said. 'I suddenly remembered what you'd told me about her . . .'

'Oh . . . yeah . . . !' muttered Margo, not quite believing him.

'But listen, Margo, I've *got* to get her into the act,' he continued, frowning seriously. 'I'm going to build a whole gigantic, colossal, travelling magic show around her and her Super-powers. So I've *got* to get her, I've just *got* to . . . !'

Meanwhile, Super Gran, Willard and Edison had arrived at Tornmouth, on the south coast. They reached the local Muttlin's camp on the Saturday and, after being shown to their chalets, they met Dave, one of the Marooncoats, who organized the sports and games for the children and adults at the Centre.

'Ah, Super Gran?' He went to shake hands with her, then drew back, pretending to be scared of getting his hand mangled. He had heard all about her Super-strength! 'I believe you put on some good shows up in Slackpool? We've heard all about it.'

'Aye, laddie. I demonstrated my Super-strength – and my Super-everything else!' She laughed.

'Well, *we* hoped you'd maybe do something different here,' Dave smiled. 'Help us in some of our competitions, perhaps?'

'Sure, laddie, whatever you like. What did you have in mind? You see, *I* can do *anything* . . . !'

'I'll bet you can!' he laughed. 'But I don't know yet. I'll think of something and let you know. Okay?'

But it didn't take long for Dave to get his idea. In fact, it happened on Super Gran and company's first morning, at breakfast in the dining-room. And it was all because the head chef was off, ill – and one of his young apprentices couldn't make porridge!

9   Porridge Pochlin'

Alf, the apprentice chef, wasn't terribly skilled in making porridge. In fact, he had only recently started work and he wasn't terribly skilled even at boiling water! So the porridge he made was a thick, lumpy mess – the lumps resembling cricket balls in size and weight! And what's more, he misread his instructions that morning!

Someone had put a tick (√), badly, in front of the figure 500, making it look like 1500. So Alf had made enough porridge for 1500 people, instead of for 500!

For a time Super Gran had gone off porridge, but now she was back on it again, and if *she* ate it she reckoned that Willard and Edison should eat it too!

'It's good for you,' she told them. 'Remember how it gave me my strength back when I lost my Super-powers in London?'

'Yes, but we don't *like* porridge!' Willard and Edison said, making faces at having to eat it. But she insisted!

'And *we* don't have Super-strength, anyway,' Edison pointed out, triumphantly. 'So it can't make much difference to *us*, can it?'

'Aye, lassie, but you've got *ordinary* strength,' Super Gran said. 'And you need to keep up all you've got for this touring round the country we're doing.'

'Huh!' the children muttered, making faces and bravely taking a mouthful.

'Oh, I think I forgot to lock the chalet,' Super Gran said. 'I'd better go back and check it, just in case . . .'

It was just as she left the dining-room that Willard and Edison discovered how bad the porridge really was. They came across the lumpy bits and they did more than make faces at them. They groaned, screwed up their faces, said, 'Yeugh!' – and took steps to get rid of it!

And it was Edison, strangely enough, who started it! She lifted the biggest, heaviest, worst lump of porridge out of her plate, turned towards the open window at her back – and flicked it off her spoon on to the grass outside!

'Hey! That's a good idea, Ed!' Willard said as he did the same, adding: 'But I bet I can flick it farther than you!' Which he proceeded to do, hitting the side wall of a nearby chalet in the process.

At this, one of the other boys at their table decided to do likewise and he also lifted the biggest, ugliest lump off *his* plate and flicked it out of the window. He was trying to beat Willard's record flick, to put it right *past* the chalet.

In no time the other people at their table, boys *and* girls – and Dads! – were joining in. And then some other people near by left their tables to come over to the open window and join in – all attempting to beat the previous records!

Soon people – mainly Dads! – were converging on the window from all over the dining-room to have a go

at chucking their porridge lumps out, each trying to be the champion porridge-chucker! And by now spoons had been discarded in favour of throwing the lumps by hand.

There was a growing mound of porridge lumps splattered all over the grassy area between the chalets. But this, luckily, would be cleared up by the sudden invasion of a flock of ever-hungry seagulls. Some of them daringly dodged the flying lumps while attempting to scoff this manna from heaven; but others, more timid, hovered in the air, waiting for the 'bombing' to stop before devouring the nauseous nosh!

Meanwhile Super Gran, returning from her chalet, met Dave the Marooncoat, on his way in for breakfast. And Dave told her all about young Alf making the lumpy porridge.

'Imagine making enough for fifteen hundred people!' he said. 'I ask you, what on earth is the kitchen staff going to do with all those lumps? They'll just have to be thrown out . . . !'

'Humph!' said Super Gran in disgust. 'They're *being* thrown out!'

For she and Dave had entered the dining-room and walked right into this scene of porridge-tossing.

'Look at that!' she said. 'It's a waste of good porridge, so it is!'

'But it's *not* good porridge, that's what I was telling you,' Dave explained. 'It's that horrible lumpy stuff. And it looks as if they're having a competition to see who can throw it the far – Hey, wait a minute . . . !'

His eyes lit up. He was having his good idea!

Super Gran left him to go over to the window and scold the porridge-chuckers for wasting good food. And, apart from a few who muttered, 'But it *isn't* good food!', the porridge-chuckers – and especially the Dads! – turned away from the window to slink back to their respective tables like naughty schoolboys!

'You should be ashamed of yourselves,' she said, standing, hands on hips, frowning at them. Then she took one hand off her hip to wag a scolding finger. 'Humph! What a waste . . . !'

Suddenly a whistle blew, the hubbub of voices in the dining-room died down and everyone turned towards the stage at one end of the room. Super Gran had been too busy being annoyed at the waste of 'good' food to notice that Dave had climbed on to the platform. He stopped whistling and put his hand up for silence.

'I've just had an idea,' he announced. 'For a new Muttlin's competition, for a way in which our honoured guest Super Gran can help us – and a super way to get rid of fifteen hundred unwanted portions of rotten, lumpy porridge! We'll have a porridge-throwing competition! But *out*side, this time!'

Everyone thought this was a good idea. It was a good way to get rid of all the sticky, yeucky, gooey lumps that *no* one – including Super Gran! – wanted to eat. For she, by this time, had tasted it and her opinion of it was:

'Yeuch! You're right, Dave! This would scunner you!'

The children thought the competition was a good idea. The Dads thought it was a good idea. And Super

Gran thought it was a good idea, and especially when Dave flattered her by saying:

'I'm sure Super Gran'll be able to throw *her* porridge lumps for *miles*!'

'We-ell, I don't know about *miles*, exactly,' she grinned modestly – for once!

'But you will give us a demonstration, won't you?' he went on. 'To show us all just how far you *can* throw them?'

'Of course, laddie. Just try and stop me!' she grinned.

'Yeah,' Willard added, 'just try and stop her showin' off!'

'We'll get the kitchen staff to drain the liquid out of the porridge and leave the lumps,' Dave went on. 'And we'll have separate competitions, for boys, girls, Mums and Dads.' He laughed. 'We mustn't miss out the Dads, must we? There were more Dads having a go at porridge-chucking than *kids*, just then!'

'Hoi! How about us grannies!' said Super Gran, pretending to be indignant. 'Don't leave the poor old grannies out of things, laddie!'

'Yeah, okay – agreed,' Dave laughed. 'And one for grannies.'

'Excuse me – just a minute . . . !'

Everyone turned to look at the tall, bearded, kilted Scotsman who stood up at the back of the room. As he proceeded to march between the tables towards the stage, he said:

'We've already got a sport like this up in Scotland. It's called "Porridge Pochlin'".' He pronounced the word 'pochlin'' to rhyme with 'loch-lin', and by now he had climbed on to the platform beside Dave. 'And we do it to raise money for charity.'

'I've never heard of that,' Super Gran said. 'That's a new one on me!'

'The *sport* may be new,' the man went on dramatically, 'but its *roots* are old – they're steeped in history.'

The diners – still only halfway through breakfast, after all! – were in no mood, right then, for history lessons. But they were going to get them anyway! The man had got their attention and he was eager to show off his knowledge!

'Aye, Porridge Pochlin',' he said, a faraway look in his eye, 'won a battle, they say ...' He was relishing his moment in the spotlight and was taking his time. 'During the Jacobite Rebellion, back in 17 ... er ... er ... back in 17-something-or-other ... Sassenach Redcoats had been trying to catch the Jacobites by surprise one morning. But the Scots, not having their weapons to hand, threw chunks o' porridge at them – that's the way they made porridge in those days, you see? And the English turned and fled! For they'd never encountered this fearful new missile before, you understand. Never!'

The man had been getting more and more dramatic with every word as he told his story, but now he ended:

'So you see, it was very very handy that the Scots had the porridge beside them, ready to eat, just as they were attacked. Aye, very handy ...'

'Yeah, mate,' a camper called out, 'an' it's lucky they weren't eating cornflakes, innit? 'Cos *they* wouldn't't've been much good as missiles, would they?'

Dave held his hand up. 'Maybe some of our competition winners'll be able to beat the record for this ... er ... "Porridge ... *Pock*lin'", was it ...?'

'No!' thundered the Scot, right into Dave's face, his beard almost touching Dave's nose, correcting his pronunciation, 'it's "*poch*lin'", "*poch*lin'"' ... And another thing,' he continued, 'to come within the rules of the official sports body – the Ancient Order of Porridge Pochlers – the "pochle", the throw, can only be done by an under-arm method and the contestants must stand still, they mustn't take a jump or a run-up to the throwing area, understand?'

By this time no one knew whether the Scot was having them on or not, but it didn't really matter, for Dave was having another of his ideas. Extracting his nose from the Scotsman's beard, he said:

'Maybe Super Gran'll not only beat the record for the Ancient Order of ... thingies! – she might even end up in the Guinness Book of Records!'

'Very probably, laddie!' Super Gran replied, immodestly as usual.

Later that morning when everyone had gathered on the sports field, either to take part in the competitions or merely to spectate, Super Gran gave a rather 'gentle' demonstration of her Super-throwing powers – or, on this occasion, her Super-pochlin' powers!

She didn't go 'all out', but held herself in check. For

Dave warned her it might discourage the contestants if she did *too* well, threw the lumps too far – and gave everyone a showing-up! The Dads, especially, who thought they were he-men, might not take part in the contest when they saw a little old lady throwing the lumps a terrific distance which they might not be able to match!

So Super Gran had to content herself with waiting until the end of the competition, until the boys, girls, Mums, Dads and grannies had all had a go, and until all the records had been established. And *then* she got to work!

The best throw, up till then, had been thirty metres, but that was nothing to Super Gran! She just took a deep breath, aimed – and threw. And *her* 'pochle' landed half the distance farther on, at forty-five metres!

'Wow!' said Willard.

'Wow!' echoed Edison. And:

'Wow-ow . . . !' said everyone else – the contestants and spectators who were lined up on each side of the throwing area, watching.

'Och! It was nothing!' said Super Gran modestly, as everyone applauded.

'Tell you what,' said Dave afterwards, 'I think you should have a go at setting a record for the Guinness Book of Records. What do you think?'

'Yeah, Gran. Try that!' Willard urged.

'Aye, well, all right then,' she agreed. 'What do I have to do?'

'While I arrange for the Record people to come and

witness your throw,' Dave said thoughtfully, 'you could spend some time in practice . . .'

'What? Practice?' Super Gran cut in, offended. 'I don't *need* practice!'

'No,' explained Dave, 'what I meant was – the more you practise, the farther you'll be able to throw it. Yes?'

'Aye, I suppose you're right,' she admitted.

Then Dave had another idea. He was full of ideas! 'In fact, if you made your official world-record attempt not here in the camp, but down in Tornmouth, you'd get more publicity for it. And I know you like publicity!'

'In Tornmouth?'

'Yes. If you did it down in the Gardens. The ones that start at the pier and cut through the town centre to the back,' he explained. 'Everyone in Tornmouth'll come along and see you, and not just the Muttlin campers. And you'll probably get your photo in the papers and everything.'

'Sounds great, Dave,' she enthused. She just *loved* getting her photo in the papers and showing off. After all, for seventy years of her life she *hadn't* been famous – so she was making up for it now! 'But maybe I'd better have a wee bit of practice in the Gardens first. Before I attempt the record, eh?'

'Right,' said Dave. 'And don't worry about a shortage of porridge lumps to practise on, 'cos we've still got thousands left!'

So a couple of days later, after Dave had received permission from the local authority, Super Gran went down into Tornmouth, to the Gardens, to practise. And with her went Willard and Edison – each armed with a large plastic bag full of lumps! – and a number of Muttlin's campers, all eager to see her in action. Then, starting at the back of the Gardens, she took her stance, ready to throw her first 'pochle'.

The arrangement was that she would throw the first lump from the back of the Gardens, then the second one from where the first one landed, and the third from where the second one landed, and so on. And she would gradually work her way from the back of the town, down the little valley which cut through the town centre and on down to the front of the Gardens, near the pier.

So she began. She threw the first lump a fair distance and then, accompanied by Willard, Edison and the campers, she hurried along to where it had landed, smashed on the ground. Then she threw the second lump and again they all trooped after it, to throw the third one.

But after she'd done this a few times, working her way through the town centre and under a bridge carrying the road from the shops at one side of the Gardens to the shops at the other side, she threw one more porridge lump – and tragedy struck! She hit someone with it!

She hit, and knocked out, a weedy little man with thin, gingery hair and a clean-shaven face . . .

10   Mystico's Disguise

The little man wore a white tee-shirt and blue faded jeans and he had suddenly popped out from behind the shrubbery at the side of the Gardens. He appeared to have been pointing a camera in her direction, and Super Gran wondered, as she rushed to see what damage she had done, if perhaps he was a Press photographer taking an action shot of her.

'Jings!' she cried as she ran. 'What've I done to the poor wee soul? I hope I haven't *hurt* him! Mercy me, I hope I haven't *killed* him! Jings, I hope I haven't broken his camera . . . !'

Suddenly – a girl with a mop of bright orange, punk-style hair came diving out of the shrubbery. She grabbed the camera-like object, shoved it into her shoulder-bag – and dived back into the shrubbery again, as quick as lightning.

'Huh?' said Super Gran, then: 'Stop – thief . . . !'

She reached the moaning man on the ground and she stopped. She was undecided what to do. Should she go after the girl thief – or attend to the injured man?

She decided that the thief would just have to escape, on this occasion, for the little man might be badly injured.

'Aw, poor wee soul,' she murmured, looking down

at him. 'I hope he's not badly hurt. I wonder who he is – and what that rotten punky girl stole off him?'

'Who is he, Gran?' asked Willard, who had come running down the Gardens after her and had just arrived.

Edison, as usual, had lagged behind and, also as usual, had tripped while running – so she was just picking herself up, some distance behind Willard.

'I don't know. That's what I was thinking myself . . . hey, that's an idea! Thinking! Maybe I could read his mind and find out who he is, eh?'

Meanwhile, a short time before this, Mystico and Margo had been chugging their way into Tornmouth and looking for somewhere to stay. They had taken about three days to complete the journey from Slackpool – their van having broken down four times on the motorway!

On arrival they had bought a local newspaper, to locate a likely theatre whose manager they could hypnotize. But the first thing they read in it was the news that Super Gran was practising in the Gardens that day for her porridge pochlin' world-record attempt.

'This couldn't be better,' Mystico said. 'She's playing right into our hands.'

'Huh? What do you mean?'

'This'll save us going out and looking for her, or sneaking into the Tornmouth Muttlin's camp to hypnotize her.' He paused, to give the situation some thought. 'We must hypnotize her as soon as possible. And here's what we're going to do . . .'

He outlined his plan to the girl, then added: 'You can wear that orange punk wig you've got, as a disguise. In case you're spotted.'

'I'm *not* spotted,' Margo denied huffily, gazing into her hand-mirror and passing her fingers over her smooth cheeks. 'I've got a *lovely* complexion!'

'Not *that* kind of "spotted", silly!'

'But what about *you*?' she asked. 'Aren't *you* going to disguise yourself?'

'I don't need to. I *am* disguised already, the way I am!'

'Huh?' Margo looked at him, puzzled.

'*My* disguise will be my *non*-disguise!' he said. 'And it was all *your* idea!'

'*My* idea?' Margo was even more puzzled. 'Why, what did *I* say?'

'*You* said how different I looked when I wasn't wearing my stage gear, remember? That my top hat made me look taller? Well, Super Gran has only seen me *in* my stage gear – my hat and cloak, false moustache and beard – and they're all *black*. But I'm not wearing *them*, I'm wearing *ordinary*, off-stage clothes – and *no* face fungus! So she'll never recognize me. Do you see now?'

'Oh – yes!' said Margo in admiration, as she looked at the light-coloured clothes he was wearing instead of his usual black, sombre stage gear.

'Clever, eh?' he said, grinning.

And so, while Super Gran had been porridge pochlin' down the valley of the Gardens, Mystico and Margo had been skulking behind the shrubbery, awaiting her approach, ready to jump out and hypnotize her. And when Mystico had accidentally got in the way of the porridge lump – resulting in his *head* getting a lump! – and been knocked out, Margo, with great presence of mind, had jumped out and retrieved the Hypnotizer before Super Gran got her hands on it.

Mystico would be proud of her, she thought, as she ran through the shrubbery, then up the slope at the side of the Gardens, out of the gate at the top and into the main shopping centre to lose herself amongst the shoppers. But then, satisfied that Super Gran hadn't pursued her, she sneaked cautiously back to the railings which surrounded the Gardens, to see what was going on.

And what was going on was that Super Gran, wondering who the 'poor wee soul' was, had read his mind – and found out that it was:

'Magic Ian . . . ! It's Mystico . . . !'

'Huh?' said Willard. 'But it *can't* be! That's nothing *like* Magic Ian!'

'What? Magic Ian?' said Edison, as incredulous as Willard, when she reached them, breathless, with a crowd of Muttlin's campers.

But Super Gran explained how different he looked without his black stage clothes and top hat. 'And that moustache and beard he wears must be false,' she muttered. 'I never thought of that.'

Seeing that he was *still* lying on the ground, moaning feebly, she reckoned he might be badly hurt and thought she'd better do something about it. So she hoisted him on to her shoulder.

'Where's the nearest hospital?' she asked the crowd of campers and spectators who had formed a circle round them.

A woman pointed up the slope towards the shops, at the side of the Gardens where Margo was hanging about. 'Up there. It's not far. You can't miss it!'

So Super Gran, carrying the now groaning Mystico, and Willard and Edison – carrying the porridge lumps! – made their way up the slope to the Gardens' exit, heading for the hospital.

'But who was that girl, Gran?' Willard asked, as they hurried along. 'The one with the punky orange hair. The one you were shoutin' at?'

'The thief? Who stole the ... hey, wait a minute – of course! Margo ...!'

'Margo?'

'And she must've been picking up the Hypnotizer!' Super Gran said. Everything suddenly fell into place. She had been too busy thinking about the 'poor wee soul' earlier to think about anything else! 'So they're still trying to hypnotize me, are they! Well, we'll just have to be on our guard, that's all.'

'But why don't you just get Dad's Hypnotizer back?' Edison asked. 'Then you wouldn't need to worry about *them*.'

'I will, lassie, don't you worry!' Super Gran said determinedly. 'It's one thing them *having* it – but it's another thing letting them use it on *me*!'

'Well at least you've got Magic Ian,' Willard said,

pointing to the unconscious man draped over her shoulder.

'Aye, that's right, and I'm going to hold on to him. I'm not going to let him out of my sight till he tells me where Margo is, with the Hypnotizer.'

'Here's the hospital,' said Edison, putting an end to the conversation.

Margo had been watching all this from the safety of the railings at the top of the Gardens, as Super Gran and company brought her boss up the slope and along the road, past the shops, to the hospital. And, although they didn't realize it, she had been following them to see what happened.

Super Gran was instructed to deposit Mystico on a bed, in a side-room of the hospital's Accident Department. Then she rejoined the others in the waiting-room, where they were giving details to a nurse.

'What d'you mean, the old lady knocked him out with porridge?' said the nurse incredulously. 'Was it still in the saucepan, or what?' She just couldn't believe it! 'I've dealt with some pretty strange accidents in my time here, but never one where the patient's been hit by porridge!'

'Then you couldn't've been helpin' the Redcoats against the Jacobites in 17-something-or-other or you'd've known all about it!' said Willard – proving that he'd been listening to the Scotsman's history lesson!

'Pardon? Are you trying to be funny?' asked the nurse.

'It was these, lassie,' Super Gran said, lifting a handful of large, hard porridge lumps out of Edison's plastic bag.

'Then I'm not surprised he was knocked out,' said

the nurse. 'Imagine throwing things like *that* about!'

She left them in the waiting-room while she went to the side-room to attend to Mystico's injuries.

'What are we waitin' for, Gran?' Willard asked.

'To make sure the wee bachle's all right,' she replied. 'And I want to ask him where Margo is – with the Hypnotizer.' She was determined now to retrieve the machine. 'We'll wait here until he's fit enough to talk to us, then we'll . . .'

But Super Gran got no farther. The nurse came rushing back into the waiting-room to announce: 'He's gone! The patient's gone! The window's open . . . !'

So they'd lost him after all!

Margo, skulking about in shrubberies for the second time that day, had been in the hospital grounds for a few minutes. She'd been wondering what to do, when she suddenly saw Mystico appear – hale and hearty, apparently! – at a ground-floor window. Then while she watched he opened it, clambered out, dropped to the ground and ran towards her.

'Come on, Margo – run . . . !'

'But – are you all right?' she asked, as she emerged from the shrubbery and ran with him out through the hospital gateway.

'Sure, I'm fine . . . !' he said, grinning.

'But – that was a quick recovery! I mean, you were unconscious just a few minutes ago!'

'Don't you believe it! I was only "out" for a few seconds at the start,' he explained, as they ran along the road towards the shops. 'I came to just as Super

Gran reached me in the Gardens. I moaned a bit to make her think I was badly hurt, so that she wouldn't go after you and the Hypnotizer. I made her think of the patient – her "poor wee soul" – rather than the thief – you! I gambled on her taking *me* to the hospital, instead of taking *you* to the police station! And it worked! She did! So that kept the Hypnotizer safe . . .' He stopped running and looked at Margo, frowning. 'It *is* safe, isn't it?'

She opened her shoulder-bag and showed him the Hypnotizer safely inside. 'Yeah, no problem.'

'I pretended I was worse than I was,' Mystico went on. 'I moaned and groaned a bit every now and then, to convince her! I knew I'd never make a getaway otherwise. I could never out-run her! It was easier escaping from the hospital!'

They ran into a large store and merged with the crowds where Super Gran, if she pursued them, would never find them. They hadn't succeeded, this time, in hypnotizing Super Gran. But there would be other days. They'd try again.

'But we'll have to watch out,' Mystico warned Margo. 'She's determined to get the Hypnotizer back.'

Meanwhile, back at the hospital, Super Gran was reacting to the news of Mystico's disappearing act – a better disappearing act than he'd ever done on stage, as a magician!

'The wee scunner!' she cried. 'The rotten wee scunnery bachle! He would sicken your chicken!'

The nurse raised her eyebrows in surprise. She

wondered what exactly was going on with all these strange people! Men being knocked out by porridge! Girls carrying large lumps of porridge about in plastic bags! Men being carried about by little old ladies with Scottish accents! Boys talking about Jacobites and Redcoats! Men patients recovering and climbing out of hospital windows! Little old ladies using strange, Scottish-sounding words! It was all very mysterious, she thought!

'Humph!' Super Gran went on. 'He's slipped through my fingers. But I'll get my *hands* on him the next time he shows his *face*, so I will!'

'Oh well, Super Gran,' Edison said, looking at her plastic bag of porridge lumps, as they left the hospital grounds, 'at least we can go back to your pochlin' practice now.'

But, as it turned out, the practice was all that Super Gran got – for she never *did* go through with her actual record attempt for the Guinness Book of Records. When they arrived back at Muttlin's, after the practice, Dave had some news for them which put the porridge pochlin' right out of their minds.

'You're due to move on to our Centre at Beastbourne next, aren't you, Super Gran?' he said.

'Aye, that's right, laddie. But not until next weekend.'

'That's what *you* think!' he beamed. 'They've fixed up a little tennis match for you. A challenge match. We all know you can't resist a challenge!'

'That's true, Dave,' she agreed. 'The only thing is – I've never really *played* tennis. Still, I suppose I'll pick it up easily enough. I pick up most things easily enough. You see, I can do *any* –'

'– thing?' smiled Dave. 'Yes, I know. I've heard!'

'But who am I playing?' she asked. 'Is it anyone I know?'

'The problem is, Super Gran,' Dave said, dodging her question, 'your opponent's going to be at Beastbourne for a big tournament, but only for *this* week. So you'll have to go there right away. Your match is on Thursday.'

'But what about the rest of my time here?' Super Gran asked. 'I've still got ten days to go.'

'Oh, don't worry about that,' Dave assured her. 'The important thing is to move on to Beastbourne. Can you manage that okay?'

'Aye, that's no bother at all,' she said. 'But you *still* haven't told me who my opponent is . . . !'

'Oh, and by the way, Beastbourne have also arranged to have a "Super Gran Look-alike" competition while you're there,' said Dave, *still* dodging Super Gran's question.

'That's nice. I'm flattered. But you *still* haven't told me who my tennis opponent is!'

'Oh . . . er . . . didn't I . . . um . . . er . . . say . . . ?' said Dave hesitantly.

'No you didn't! Come on, what's the mystery, laddie? Who's my opponent? Who is she?'

'Well . . . it's . . . er . . . ah . . . um . . . it's not a *she*, exactly – it's a *he* . . . !' he said.

'Oh, a *man* player?' Super Gran said cheerfully. 'Well, that'll be a wee bit more difficult, I suppose!'

'Oh ... ah ... um ... well, you see ... er ...'

'Come on, who is it? Spit it out! Or do I have to read your mind, eh?'

'Well ... it's ... er ... um ... Don – Don Makinrow!' he said, pronouncing the 'row' part of the name to rhyme with 'cow'.

Edison exploded. 'What? You don't mean – "Superchat" ...?'

'Well ... ah ... um ... yes, that's right,' Dave admitted.

'Superchat?' said Super Gran innocently. 'Who's Superchat?'

'Who's Superchat?' gasped Willard. 'Wow! He's only the best tennis player in the world, that's who! He's ... he's the world champion!'

11 Super Gran versus Superchat!

'We've arranged the special "Super Gran Look-alike" competition for next week,' said Suzi, one of the Beastbourne Muttlin's girl Marooncoats, when she showed Super Gran and company to their chalets. 'Is that all right?'

'Sure, lassie. As long as you only expect the competitors to *look* like me and not *act* like me! It's not everyone who has my Super-powers, you know!'

Suzi laughed. 'No, they'll only *look* like you. They'll all line up, dressed as grannies – as "Super Grans". It should be fun.'

'But never mind the "Super Gran" competition,' said Super Gran, 'tell me about the tennis match. It's tomorrow, isn't it?'

'Yes, in the tennis stadium in town, where they play *all* the big matches. I'll take you down there in a Muttlin's car.'

'Suzi,' Edison whispered, 'she hasn't got a chance. Not against the world champion. Not even *Super Gran* could play against the world champion!'

''Course she could!' Willard insisted hotly when he overheard this. 'Couldn't you, Gran?'

'Aye, of course I could!' Super Gran agreed confidently. 'Why not?'

'But you said you'd never *played* tennis before!' Edison reminded her.

'Aye, well I played a wee bit when I was a lassie, lassie!' she admitted, then laughed at her choice of words. 'Och well, it'll soon come back to me, don't worry!' *She* certainly wouldn't!

'That's the spirit, Super Gran,' Suzi encouraged. 'I'm sure you'll do fine.'

'And this Don Makinrow's called "Superchat", is he?' she said.

'That's because he talks a lot while he's playing,' Suzi explained. 'His name is quite appropriate – Makinrow – for he's always "makin' rows"!'

What Suzi *didn't* explain was that Superchat had the reputation of being not only the best tennis player in the world – but also the noisiest! He talked, chattered, shouted and bawled throughout every game he played.

He just never shut up. He talked to everyone – and *anyone*: his opponents, the umpire, the referee, the line-judges, the ball-boys, the spectators, the TV cameramen and sound recordists, the radio commentators, the Press reporters and photographers, the late-comers – everyone!

To put his opponents off their strokes, he *would* insist on talking to them over the net during the whole of the game, insisting on impressing on them that: 'I'm the world's best!'

And when he was interviewed, after another successful match – and he seldom lost a *game*, never mind a *set*, never mind a *match*! – by radio and TV interviewers, he continued to talk to *them* non-stop. So much so that the producers and directors often had to switch over to other microphones and cameras to dodge him! Not that he let them, for he'd follow the camera about, determinedly staring into it, trying to continue talking to the TV audience, whether it was still filming him or not!

So this is what Super Gran would have to put up with when she played tennis with Superchat – although she didn't know that yet!

The next day Suzi drove Super Gran, Willard and Edison into town, to the Beastbourne tennis stadium, for Super Gran's big day – her date with the world tennis champion. It was Super Gran versus Superchat!

'Hi, Super Gran!' he greeted her at the net, shaking her hand. 'How-di-do? I'm Superchat.'

'And I'm Super Gran. I'm just a poor, defenceless little old lady!'

'Yeah, you are, aren't you? This is gonna be easy!'

'And you're Makinrow?' she said. 'Aye, and I believe you always are . . .'

'Pardon?'

'Makin' rows . . . !'

'How's that again, Super Gran?'

'I was just saying – you're always taking bows! Bowing to your fans?'

'Yeah, I sure am. I'm the greatest tennis player in the world, did you know that? In fact, I reckon I'm just about the greatest tennis star this lil ole world has ever seen! Did you know *that?*'

'I don't know about that, but I know you're a wee bit o' a blether!'

'Hey, Super Gran, you sure speak funny . . . !'

But before she could indignantly reply that the 'funny' was merely her good old Scottish accent, Superchat went on – as Superchat usually did!

'I'm the world's best . . . '

'World's *best*?' she murmured. 'It's more like the world's *pest*!'

'Pardon? How's that again?'

'I just said – let's put it to the *test*!' fibbed Super Gran.

She decided that if this was going to be a boasting match, she might as well join in! 'Do you know that *I* can do *anything*?'

'Yeah? And I'm the world's best . . . !'

'And *I* can do *anything* . . . !'

'Yeah? And I'm the world's best . . . !'

At last the match started. But, with Super*chat* boasting and with Super *Gran* boasting, it turned out to be about the noisiest tennis match on record: '*I'm* the world's *best* . . . *I* can do *anything* . . . *I'm* the world's *best* . . . *I* can do *anything* . . .' – interminably! It sounded like a record with the needle stuck in the groove!

'Och!' said Super Gran in disgust. 'You're nothing but a big blether, so you are. World's *best*? World's *boast* is more like it! What town in America do you come from – Boston? Cos "boastin'" seems to be what you're best at!'

But Superchat was more than a boaster. He really

was the world's best player, as Super Gran was just finding out!

Superchat's constant chat was gradually wearing Super Gran down – as it was intended to do! For this, after all, was how he won most of his matches, it being extremely difficult for his opponents to concentrate on their game when he chatted all through it – not to mention before and after the game as well!

But Super Gran had an additional problem. When her concentration was broken, which it was by all the chat, her Super-hearing would occasionally switch itself on, which made Superchat's chat all the louder and more annoying to *her* than it would have been to an *ordinary* player. And this, she discovered, was one of the drawbacks of being Super!

It came as no surprise, therefore, when Superchat easily won the first of three sets – by a score of six games to love! And this despite the fact that Willard, Edison, Suzi and most of the crowd were yelling, cheering and urging *her* on, rather than the noisy, bragging, off-putting Superchat.

But suddenly, out of the blue, Super Gran got an unexpected – if temporary – ally. It was none other than her enemy, Mystico – although she never realized it!

Mystico and Margo, after being unsuccessful with Super Gran in the Gardens on the Tuesday, hung about there during the whole of the Wednesday, on the chance that she'd return. But when they didn't see her they phoned Muttlin's to find out where she was likely to be contacted – and were told the news.

'What?' said a shattered Mystico. 'She's gone? To Beastbourne? But she's only been *here* a few days . . . !'

He slammed down the phone and complained to Margo: 'Curses! Bats' boots! I wish that old pest would stay in one place long enough for me to hypnotize her! Instead of traipsing all over the country like this!'

He pushed his way past Margo to get out of the phone-box, went over to his van – and kicked chunks out of it in his temper!

'Hey! Mystico!' Margo yelled, grabbing his arm and hauling him back from the poor, defenceless vehicle. 'Watch it! Remember that's got to get us to Beastbourne. And it's not likely to, if you treat it like that!'

'No . . . no, you're quite right,' he agreed, calming down. 'Sorry, van . . . !'

He was so upset he was even talking to vans now!

They returned to their hotel and packed their bags. Then Margo reminded her boss about the theatre manager – the one he'd just newly hypnotized into giving them a job for a couple of weeks.

'You'll have to go back and *un*-hypnotize him again,' she said.

'That old bat, Super Gran, is more bother than she's worth,' he grumbled.

'Does that mean you don't want to hypnotize her now, for the act?' said Margo, brightening. Maybe now she could concentrate on her *own* solo act again, instead of trailing all over the country with Mystico in pursuit of Super Gran.

'No, it doesn't. I *still* want her for the act. Even more so . . . !'

So they moved on to Beastbourne, and had just arrived in town when Margo spotted a poster advertising the tennis match between Super Gran and Superchat. She pointed to it out of the van window.

'That's it!' cried Mystico, swerving the van on to a traffic island in his excitement. 'That's the very place!'

'Huh?' said Margo. '*What's* the very place?'

'The very place to hypnotize her!' he explained. 'At the tennis match. She'll be a sitting duck. While she's on the court she can't escape – and *I* can't miss her. It couldn't be better. When does it start?'

Margo looked at her watch. 'In ten minutes . . .'

'What?' he exploded, swerving the van on to another traffic island! 'We've no time to lose. We'll have to find the stadium, park the van, buy our tickets . . .'

'And find ourselves a hotel . . .' Margo said, interrupting.

'And find ourselves a . . . never mind the hotel!' he barked. '*It* can wait till after the match. *It*'ll still be there when Super Gran's gone.'

'Yes, but spare rooms won't be,' Margo pointed out. 'There's a big tennis tournament on all week and the hotels'll be full. If we leave it too late we won't get in anywhere.'

'Oh well, okay, okay,' muttered Mystico, to shut her up. 'We'll go to the stadium and buy our tickets. Then you can go and look for rooms and join me at the tennis later. How about that?'

And so, while Mystico parked the van at the stadium's car park and took his seat in the stand, with the Hypnotizer and a clear view of his target, Margo went happily off to find them somewhere to stay.

'I'm going to be a menace at the tennis!' he gloated.

But Mystico sat through the first set, so engrossed with actually seeing the famous Superchat 'in the flesh' that he forgot what he was *there* for – to hypnotize Super Gran. But then, after that set, he realized that, against the hard-hitting, much-chatting Superchat, Super Gran didn't seem to be having much of a chance to use her Super-powers and play to the best of her ability. So, temporarily taking pity on her, he decided to even the match up a bit! He'd make it more of a game and less of a slaughter.

He aimed the Hypnotizer at Superchat and, speaking quietly into the microphone so that the spectators sitting around him – who thought he was merely taking photographs with his camera! – wouldn't hear, he told the star to shut up!

'Just concentrate on the "racquet" instead of the "racket"!' he told him. Then, pleased with his little bit of jokey word-play, he added: 'Concentrate on the "ball" – and never mind the "bawl"!' He giggled quietly to himself at his ready wit.

He decided that after Super Gran had had the chance to play to her full potential in the second set he'd do what he'd come to do, hypnotize her, towards the end of it. After all, he didn't want to miss his golden opportunity, having Super Gran as a sitting target like that.

And 'sitting', he reckoned, was probably the best time to get her, when she was sitting down at the change-over of ends, having a drink of orange.

Superchat, meanwhile, had just been hypnotized. He had been right in the middle of his usual boast: 'I'm the world's be –', when it happened. He was suddenly struck dumb!

Silence reigned. The whole stadium was enveloped in a sudden hush which it hadn't experienced since Superchat hit town! And everyone was astonished: Willard, Edison and Suzi in the stand in front of Mystico, the crowd, the umpire, the ball-boys, the line-judges, the TV cameramen, the sound recordists, the radio commentators, the Press reporters and photographers, the late-comers, Super Gran – and especially Superchat himself!

Everyone was amazed to see – or rather, to hear! – the second set being played in complete, utter silence. In fact, you could have heard the proverbial pin dropping. Cameras popped all over the place at the open-mouthed look of shocked surprise on the world champion's face.

Superchat, taken aback by this inexplicable bolt from the blue, couldn't do a thing right. He mis-hit his shots, he messed up his serves and he was so dazed that he couldn't, without help, even find his way back to his seat for a drink of orange during change-overs!

But Super Gran, although as puzzled by Superchat's sudden silence as everyone else, decided to take advantage of it. After all, *he* had taken advantage of *her* with all his chat earlier, so why shouldn't she get her own back now?

So, taking her chance when she got it, Super Gran served Super-aces on each of her serves, and Super-returned each of *his* serves – that is, the few serves he managed to hit over the net! And she quickly and easily beat the confused, silent, non-bragging, non-blethering Superchat – by six games to love!

'Hooray! Good old Gran!' shouted Willard above the volume of cheers which rang round the stadium.

'Wow!' said Edison disbelievingly. 'Did you see that? Six–love?'

'We *knew* you could do it, Super Gran!' yelled Suzi, jumping up and down in her seat with the rest of the crowd in her excitement.

'Now then, me beauties,' muttered Mystico to himself in his seat a few rows farther back, 'each of you has had the advantage over the other. So let's see who wins the third set, shall we ... ?' And he sniggered as he said this, for he was reverting to his usual nasty!

He cancelled his instructions to Superchat so that the world champion would be able to speak again and would return to his usual noisy self. And at the same time he moved the Hypnotizer so that it was aiming at Super Gran instead.

For this was his big moment – the moment he had waited for. The moment for which he had pursued Super Gran from Slackpool to Tornmouth to Beastbourne. And he revelled in his moment of power.

'He, he, he!' he gloated, mentally rubbing his hands together.

She'd had her little moment of glory. She'd had her chance to even the score with Superchat. She'd had her chance to become famous by winning a set against him – which was more than most of his opponents ever did! – and at six–love, too! And her just a little old lady! What more did she want? What more could she ask for?

But now, for Mystico, it was back to business – *nasty* business! He took careful aim at Super Gran sitting in her chair, drinking her orange juice – and he pressed the button.

Super Gran was just about to be hypnotized . . . !

12 Two Super Grans Too Many!

Mystico took careful aim at Super Gran, pressed the button – and tragedy struck! But it didn't strike Super Gran, it struck Mystico! And it struck in the shapely shape of the ever-faithful – Margo!

She had found a small hotel near by with two vacant rooms, without much trouble, and had entered the stadium and located Mystico in the stand. She now shuffled along the row and sat down heavily beside him. 'It's me. I've arrived. I've booked the hotel.'

But in the process of sitting down she accidentally jostled Mystico's arm, making him miss his aim at Super Gran, who was back on court again ready to serve – and causing the rays to hit the umpire instead!

'Get lost, will you!' Mystico angrily barked at Margo – or, at least, he meant to bark it at Margo! But the umpire climbed down out of his high tennis chair and walked across the court to obey the command!

'Huh?' said Super Gran, down on the court as the man walked directly in front of one of her Super-serves – which, luckily, missed him by centimetres!

'Where's he going? What's the matter? What's going on?' asked the puzzled buzz of spectators' voices.

Margo decided she was hungry and rose out of her seat

again. 'I'm going for an ice cream, Mystico. Do you want one?'

'Curses! Gnats' knickers!' Mystico muttered, annoyed at being disturbed as he aimed at Super Gran again. He also wondered, like everyone else, where the umpire was striding off to. 'Do what you like! Go for ice creams! Get a dozen, if you want . . . !'

The umpire, in obedience to Mystico's command, 'Do what you like!', did a handstand, followed by a few cartwheels, on the centre of the court! Then he headed towards the refreshments tent at the back of the stand.

There was a lull in the game for a few minutes while Super Gran and Superchat wondered whether or not to proceed. The hubbub of puzzled murmurs from the crowd continued, and increased in volume.

Mystico took aim on Super Gran, who was at a temporary standstill, but Superchat got in the way as he tried to discuss the situation with her. Not that Superchat was chatting a lot! For the shock of his sudden dumbness had affected him so badly that he was scared to speak too much in case it happened again!

'Curses! Pigs' pyjamas!' Mystico moaned. 'Foiled again!'

The umpire suddenly reappeared – with a tray containing a dozen ice cream cones! He handed one each to the players, then went round presenting the rest to the ball-boys and line-judges. He took the last one himself and clambered back up on to his high chair to restart the game!

Mystico, when he eventually had a clear sight on

Super Gran again, aimed and pressed the button. But Margo unfortunately chose that exact moment to return to her seat with their two ices – and again disturbed him. He was fated!

'Sorry, boss,' she said cheerfully, not fully realizing what she'd done.

'Sit down, will you!' snapped Mystico, as he again missed Super Gran and 'sprayed' the rays over the ball-boys – who instantly sat down!

They sat at the sides and ends of the court, in the positions they'd been in, waiting, crouched, to recover the balls hit out of play. And they refused to get up again when told to by the umpire, the referee, the line-judges, Super Gran, the spectators and Superchat – silently gesturing! They just wouldn't budge!

In fact, the only way they could clear the ice-cream-eating boys off the edges of the court was to lift them bodily – still in their 'sitting' positions – and carry them away, so that the game could proceed!

Margo, meanwhile, was urgently thrusting Mystico's rapidly melting ice cream at him. But he was too busy lining up Super Gran in the Hypnotizer's view-finder to be bothered with it. So this made him miss his aim once again – and he hit a large section of the crowd behind her at the side of the arena, alongside the umpire.

'Oh, go take a jump!' he yelled. At Margo – he thought!

But suddenly the newly hypnotized section of the crowd jumped out of their seats, ran down the steps to the court and proceeded to obey Mystico's command. They took a jump – lots of jumps – all over the grass, much to the astonishment of the other spectators and much to the horror of the stadium officials, seeing their sacred turf being ruined before their very eyes!

And so, once again, the match was held up.

But this 'war dance' by crazy British tennis fans was the last straw for Superchat. It had all been too much for him and he'd been put off his game completely! Not to mention being put off chatting for life! In fact, Super-chat never really lived up to his nickname after that match with Super Gran. He became known, ever afterwards, as the quiet, shy, retiring, modest man of tennis!

But if Superchat had been put off *his* game, Super Gran certainly hadn't been put off *her* game. As soon as the hypnotized spectators had been ushered off the court and had returned to their seats, the match was resumed for the umpteenth time – and Super Gran took command! Taking advantage of Superchat being off his stroke, she Super-served, Super-volleyed, Super-lobbed and Super-backhanded every shot – and won the third set by six games to three.

She had won! The battle of Super Gran versus Super-chat ended in a victory for the little old lady, who told her defeated opponent (who had long since stopped saying, 'I'm the world's best'):

'Listen, laddie, you're *not* the world's best – *I* am! Didn't I tell you I could do *anything*? And me just a poor, defenceless little old lady, too!'

'Good old Super Gran!' shouted Edison, above the sounds of the cheering crowd and the popping Press photographers' cameras.

'I *knew* she'd do it!' added Willard gleefully. 'I *told* you so!'

'Hooray! Good on you, Super Gran!' yelled Suzi.

The crowd thought it was great to see a frail-looking old lady beating a strapping, athletic tennis player like Makinrow. It was just magic, they thought. And so did the kids in the crowd who began to chant:

'Su-per Gran is ma-gic ... ! Su-perchat is tragic ...!'

Up in the stand, Margo was asking: 'What's the matter?' – as her boss ground his teeth in rage, threw his ice cream to the floor of the stand, left his seat and stomped off, furious and frustrated.

'What's wrong with your ice?' she called after him. 'Was it the wrong flavour or what ...?'

Mystico had lost his chance at the sitting duck. He had missed Super Gran, repeatedly, with the Hypnotizer and now the spectators had flooded on to the court and were surrounding her, slapping her back and congratulating her. Not to mention the journalists and photographers who were crowding round her, interviewing her for the Press, radio and television.

There was no way that Mystico could aim the Hypnotizer's beam past all of *them* without hitting the wrong people – again! He'd had it.

But he was angrier at himself for having been softhearted enough to give Super Gran that chance in the second set. He should just have let her take her chances with Superchat and not interfered. And *he* should have taken *his* chances when he'd got them, and didn't.

Then, on top of that, to have Margo continually jost-ling and disturbing him, and now the crowd was block-ing his view. It just wasn't his day! He was off. He'd just have to try for another chance at hypnotizing her, some other time.

The next few days were comparatively quiet. Super Gran took a while to get over her excitement at 'hypno-tizing' the crowd with her tennis display. And Mystico took a while to get over his disappointment at hypno-tizing no one *but* the crowd!

But then, the following Monday was the day of the Muttlin's 'Super Gran Look-alike' competition, which Super Gran – with a little help from her friends Willard and Edison – was going to judge. So after lunch the three of them came out to the playing field which was situated in a square, surrounded on each side by chalets.

They made their way into the crowd of onlooking campers and Marooncoats, who opened up to let them through to the contestants and Suzi.

'Ah, there you are, Super Gran! Hi, Willard, Edison,' she greeted them. 'Are you ready?' She stood beside the twelve contestants, her clip-board with the details in her hands, ready to start the competition.

'Remember – Robert ... ?' she whispered to Super Gran as she approached.

Super Gran nodded. Robert was one of the Maroon-coats who, dressed as a clown, had a part to play at the end of the contest.

Super Gran glanced along the line of competitors and smiled at the way they were all dressed up to look like her, with their tartan tammies, strings of white beads, lilac cardigans, green and red floral dresses and handbags. But if she had used her X-ray eyes, or her mind-reading, to look through the disguises, she would have realized that a couple of imposters had sneaked into the line-up amongst the genuine camping contestants!

Mystico had decided to have another go at hypnotizing Super Gran and when he'd heard about the 'Super Gran Look-alike' competition he'd decided that that was his chance. He and Margo gained admittance to Muttlin's on buying two 'day' tickets, which allowed outsiders into the camp for one day only. Then, in the car park, they had taken turns in the back of the van to put on their 'Super Gran Look-alike' costumes.

'Oh-oh!' muttered Margo, looking down at her string of white beads. 'The string's a bit frayed. I hope it doesn't break.'

'Oh, don't worry about *that*!' Mystico told her. 'A little thing like that's not going to upset *our* plans!' He laughed.

But he was wrong! It did!

Suzi noted their names on her clip-board, then they lined up with the other, genuine, Super Gran Look-alikes, with Margo near the centre of the line and Mystico – in 'drag' – at the far end of it.

He planned to use the Hypnotizer as Super Gran walked along the line, judging them, and he was hiding it behind his handbag!

'Ladies and gentlemen, boys and girls ...' Suzi announced. 'Super Gran would like to look at her look-alikes – all of whom are very, very good – and judge which of them is best. Okay, Super Gran ...? It's all yours!'

Edison whispered: 'Are all these people aunts?'

'Aunts?' Super Gran said. 'No, they're supposed to be grans. Why?'

'Oh,' Edison joked, 'I just thought they were supposed to be contest-*aunts*, that's all!' She giggled.

'Oh, there's Robert,' Super Gran whispered back. 'Pretend you don't see him!'

'I *don't* see him!' Willard said – loudly! – looking all round. 'Where is he?'

'Shhh! He's hiding at the side of that chalet, over there,' his Gran whispered out of the side of her mouth. 'Don't look round!'

Suzi had arranged for Robert, in his clown's costume, to sneak out from the side of the chalet when everyone's attention was firmly on the contest. Then he'd come up behind Super Gran when the judging was completed and pelt her with a couple of custard pies – one in each hand, hidden behind his back.

As Super Gran, Willard and Edison moved along the line, conferring with each other as they went, Mystico suddenly made a slight change of plan. He got greedy. He decided that, as well as hypnotizing Super Gran, he should get Margo the prize for being the best Super Gran look-alike. After all, it was a cash prize and the money would help to pay for the 'day tripper' admission tickets! It was simply a matter of economy!

But that was the mistake he made. And Margo's beads breaking didn't help, either!

Mystico, aiming the Hypnotizer from behind his handbag, pointed it at Super Gran as she stopped to judge the disguised Margo's costume. His whispered command was: '*That* one – the one in the red tammy – let *her* have it!' – meaning, of course, that Margo was to be declared the winner and get the prize.

But it was just then, as Mystico pressed the button, that the frayed string on Margo's beads broke, as it had threatened to do! Super Gran automatically bent down to retrieve the cascading objects – and the Hypnotizer's beam shot over her head and hit Robert the clown, sneaking up behind her with his custard pies at the ready!

Robert, hearing Mystico's command: 'Let *her* have it!' – meaning the prize – *let* her, Margo, have it! He obeyed and threw the pies at her, in quick succession, before she could duck.

While the contestants, Marooncoats, spectators, Super Gran, Willard and Suzi were all surprised by this – but howled with laughter – Edison, who had been looking elsewhere, suddenly spotted the familiar shape of the Hypnotizer sticking out from behind the handbag of the last 'Super Gran' in the line-up. And she yelled to the *real* Super Gran:

'Super Gran . . . ! Look . . . ! The Hypnotizer . . . !'

Edison didn't take time to work out if it was Mystico who was holding it, or Margo, or someone else – she just yelled! And Super Gran zoomed in her X-ray eyesight on the last 'Super Gran' in the line, saw through 'her' disguise and realized that it was in fact Mystico.

'Jings! It's Magic Ian – the wee scunner!'

She forgot all about judging the 'Super Gran' in front of her – whom she hadn't recognized yet as being Margo – in her hurry to reach Mystico and retrieve the Hypnotizer.

But Margo, the pie-covered 'Super Gran' in front of her, tripped her up as she ran. And then, as Super Gran scrambled to her feet, Mystico threw his handbag at her and pushed a couple of contestants in front of her to block her advance. And, while Super Gran fell over them, climbed back to her feet and then stopped to help *them* to *their* feet again – Mystico made good his escape.

Seeing a boy standing near a chalet with a Muttlin's bicycle, Mystico raced across to him, pushed him aside and 'borrowed' it. He jumped on and rode off round the corner of the chalet, heading for the safety of the car park and his trusty – rusty! – old van.

'Hey – Magic Ian! Come back!' yelled Super Gran. 'Stop him, someone . . . !'

She started to pursue him but gave up when she realized he had escaped. She dashed back, instead, to confront the other 'Super Gran', the one who had tripped her up, whom she now suspected was Margo in disguise. But she was too late! For Margo, scraping custard pie off her face as she ran, had already bolted in the opposite direction to Mystico; like him, she had dodged between two chalets and was heading in the direction of the car park.

So Mystico and Margo had failed again – they'd 'blown' it. Time was running out for them. They would *have* to succeed soon – next time, perhaps . . . ?

13 Hilly Hi-jinks!

Super Gran, Willard and Edison moved on to Tar-borough, the last resort on their tour of Muttlin's Holi-day Centres, where Edison joked: '*This* is the last resort!'

Tarborough was built on a series of hills which ran down to the harbour. Behind the harbour there were a number of narrow, cobbled streets of the older, original part of town. And behind the old part *and* the newer, broader streets of the modern part of town was Bean-shome Park. The park contained, among other attrac-tions, a large lake big enough to have a 'pirate' galleon which sailed back and forth from a jetty, taking kid-dies to a 'treasure island' in the middle of the lake. And also in this park, near the lake, was Cromwell's Mount.

They were greeted on arrival at Muttlin's by Eric, one of the Marooncoats.

'Welcome, Super Gran,' he grinned nervously, excited by Super Gran's presence! 'And do we have lots of things for you to do, while you're here! You can demon-strate your Super-powers and help with the kiddies' sports and take part in some of the competitions against the Dads and . . .' He practically said it all in the one breath!

'Hey! Hold on, hold on, laddie! Give me a chance!

I know I'm Super and I can do *anything*! But I can't do *everything* – not all at once, anyway!'

Eric calmed down and explained that he was rather excited because they'd never had Super Gran in their camp before, and he wanted to make the most of it.

'In fact, come to think of it,' he grinned, 'we've never had Super *Anybody* in our camp before!'

Then he added that, as well as the events he'd already mentioned, there was another – special – event they'd like her to take part in.

'And what's so special about it, eh?' Super Gran asked with a smile.

'Well ... ah ... um ... it's a ... um ... a skateboard race ...' he said.

'Oh, is that all?' She looked all about her at the flat, level ground of the camp area and playing-fields of the Centre. 'I don't suppose it'll be all *that* strenuous, will it?'

'We-ell ... I dunno ...' Eric hesitated. 'It's against our local skateboard champion, Reg Timson. But it's not being held here in the camp. It'll take place in town, on ... ah ... um ... a hill. On ... ah ... Cromwell's Mount ...'

He hesitated, waiting for some kind of response or comment – or outburst, perhaps! – from Super Gran. But as she didn't know the town, there wasn't much she *could* say.

'Oh, so it's downhill, is it?' she replied innocently, making the understatement of the year! And Eric, the coward, decided to leave it at that for the time being

– she'd find out soon enough what Cromwell's Mount was like!

For what she didn't know was that Cromwell's Mount was not only the highest, steepest hill in town, at 135 metres, it was also full of twists, hairpin bends and dangerous curves – and was used for car and motor bike races! And it was not unknown for some contestants to take a bend too quickly and end up flying – rather than motoring! – over the edge of it, downwards. But Super Gran didn't discover this until a few days later, on the day of the race, when she arrived at the bottom of the hill to meet Reg, her opponent.

'Will you look at that!' she exclaimed, staring up at the twisty heights. 'Och well, I'll just have to get on with it, won't I? I've accepted the challenge now, so it's too late to back out.'

The idea was that they would start right at the top of the hill and race down the racing circuit to finish at the bottom, near the lake.

Willard had arranged for him and Edison to borrow a couple of Muttlin's bikes, so they could follow the race. 'And we'll take our CB radios with us,' he had suggested to Edison, who'd groaned and made a face at him.

'Oh no, not again! Must we? What do you want *them* for?'

Willard hadn't been bothering about them for some time now, and Edison had hoped he'd forgotten them altogether. But he hadn't!

'They'll come in handy durin' the race,' he said. 'I'll be followin' Gran down the hill on the bike, and you'll be waitin' down at the lakeside, at the bottom of the hill – and we can keep in contact . . .'

'How do *you* know I'll be at the bottom of the hill?' Edison asked indignantly. 'Can you foretell the future, or something!'

'No, but I know what you're like about climbin' hills,' he retorted, 'and cyclin' and runnin' and trippin' and . . .!'

'Oh, all right, don't go on and on about it,' said Edison, huffed.

But Willard had been spot on with his prediction, as it turned out. For Edison took one look at Cromwell's Mount and its winding, twisty racing-circuit road and, as Willard had suggested, decided to stay at the lakeside, at the finishing line, and listen in on her CB radio.

'Well, good luck, Super Gran,' she said, as Willard put *his* radio into its container and strung it round his neck, while Super Gran climbed into Eric's car, which would take her and Reg, and their skateboards, to the top of the hill. 'Oh, sorry! And you too, Reg – good luck!'

'Thanks,' he said, as he climbed in beside Super Gran.

'We'll see you in a wee while, lassie,' Super Gran said. 'We'll not be long in zooming back down here again!'

Presently they arrived at the top of the hill, where everyone got ready for the race. Super Gran and Reg stood beside their skateboards, while the spectators and Press reporters and photographers crowded round. Eric, who would flag them off, would then follow them down in his car; Willard, who had cycled up – although he'd had to *walk* most of the way! – hovered in the background, ready to follow them down on his bike.

But meanwhile, halfway down the hill, Mystico's van – with L-plates attached – was parked at the side of the road. Mystico and Margo had driven up in it *behind* Eric's car, so that they wouldn't be spotted. And while Margo nervously clutched the steering wheel, Mystico, beside her, nervously clutched the Hypnotizer.

By posing as a Press reporter seeking news of Super Gran, Mystico had kept track of the old lady's movements, both at Beastbourne and here at Tarborough. And in the process he'd heard about the skateboard race and quickly made plans to hypnotize Super Gran during it, halfway down the hill, where no one, apart from her opponent, would be about. That way he wouldn't hit whole crowds of people as he'd done before!

So he sat nervously waiting for the racers to appear down the hill – he was all set to hypnotize Super Gran at last!

The only problem was, he'd need Margo to drive the van for him – and she was still only a learner driver. So he gave her a few quick extra lessons – a 'crash' course, he called it, but hoped she wouldn't take the word 'crash' too literally! So this explained the L-plates and the nervous Margo, for she'd only driven on *level* roads so far. She hadn't even attempted hills, never mind a hill like Cromwell's Mount with its winding, twisting, hairpin bends!

The race started and the contestants pushed off on

their boards. Willard set off behind them on his bike and the reporters, photographers and spectators with cars set off after *him*. But Eric, after flagging the racers off, jumped into his car to follow them, discovered it wouldn't start and was left to walk down the hill with the other – pedestrian – spectators!

'They're off!' said Willard, into his radio transceiver, giving a running commentary to Edison at the lakeside. 'Gran's just ahead ... they're goin' into the first bend ... it's Reg, he's catchin' up ... now it's a straight bit ... then another twisty bit ... now a double bend ...'

He cycled along with one hand on the handlebar and the other clutching his radio. But then, as he and the racers approached the halfway point, he said:

'They're still neck-and-neck ... they're passin' a van at the side of the road ... I'm comin' up to it – help! It's Magic Ian's van! *He's* here, he must be tryin' to hypnotize Gran again ... oh-oh, she must've been hit by the ray ... she's wobblin' about a bit ... she's bumpin' into Reg ... Reg's goin' ahead ... Gran's swervin' to the side ... hey – watch out! That was Magic Ian's van! It pulled out from the side and it's zig-zaggin' about and nearly hit me when it passed! It's goin' along behind Gran and Reg ... it's beltin' back and forward across the road ... I think Margo's drivin' – she's terrible! Now Magic Ian's leanin' out the window with the Hypnotizer! He's tryin' to hit Gran with it again ...!'

And so, at long last, Mystico achieved his ambition. Not his *big* ambition, admittedly, about his magic show – that would come later – but his small ambition, to hypnotize Super Gran. So Super Gran was hypnotized.

But in the excitement of the moment, Mystico had forgotten to use the control knob at its highest setting, the one required for someone as strong as Super Gran. The result was, there wasn't enough power to put her completely under the Hypnotizer's influence, so the effects came and went; one minute she was hypnotized, and the next, she wasn't!

But Mystico didn't realize this. He was too busy being terrified out of his skull with Margo's wild, erratic driving to think clearly. Her driving on flat, level roads was bad enough, but on Cromwell's Mount – wow!

Super Gran, meanwhile, was careering crazily down the steep, twisting hill, somehow managing to keep up with Reg, but not knowing too much about what was happening or what she was doing. Then behind them came the fleet of vehicles. There was Mystico's Margo-driven van, Willard on his bike – cycling one-handed as he commentated to Edison, then the reporters, photographers and spectators in their cars.

Super Gran and Reg continued on their way down and round the curving hill. Super Gran, half-hypnotized and not quite knowing where she was going, kept bumping into Reg, who, puzzled, kept trying to keep out of her way, although he couldn't manage to get ahead of her. For Super Gran, in a semi-trance though she was, stuck to his side all the way down.

'They haven't far to go, now,' Willard informed

Edison over the radio. 'Can't you see them yet? And Magic Ian's van behind them . . . ?'

Edison, amongst the spectators at the lakeside, with her radio held to her ear, looked towards the hill. 'No, not yet . . . Oh, yes, yes . . . Here they come . . .'

Super Gran and Reg, still neck-and-neck, came zooming down into the last stretch, going faster and faster – towards the lake at the bottom. Meanwhile the 'pirate' galleon full of children heading for 'treasure island' was drawing away from the jetty near the finishing line.

'Oh-oh!' murmured Edison. 'The lake . . .! Super Gran'll go into it!'

But Super Gran *didn't* go into the lake – and neither did Reg! Well, not exactly! Super Gran nudged him as they approached the jetty and the slight collision, at speed, shot the man off to his left, so that he bounced on to the jetty. Then he zoomed across it and over the edge, sailing through the air to land – on the galleon!

'Huh . . . ? What happened? Where am I?' he muttered as he lay on the deck, surrounded by curious kiddies and a pink plastic mechanical parrot attached to the ship's rigging, which screamed at him:

'Pieces of eight, pieces of eight . . . make 'im walk the plank . . . !'

Meanwhile: 'Wee-eee-eee!' yelled Super Gran as she continued going, straight through the finishing line – without showing any signs of finishing!

She was followed by Mystico's zig-zagging van, scattering nearby spectators in every direction, which was followed, in turn, by Willard.

'Oh-oh!' cried Edison over her CB radio to Willard, before looking up to see him arriving, and passing, on his bike. 'She's not stopping! She's running right out the park . . . !'

'Yeah, I see that!' Willard shouted back to her as he went by. 'Come on, let's get after her. On your bike!'

Super Gran went zooming on down the hill outside Beanshome Park, helpless to stop herself and only now and again conscious of what she was doing, being still in her coming-and-going semi-hypnotic trance. She went along a main street, weaved in and out of the traffic in the busy High Street and then headed towards the narrow, cobbled streets of the old part of town.

And Mystico accompanied her, for Margo had managed to catch up, and for a few dozen metres drove the van alongside Super Gran while Mystico leaned out of his window again to aim the Hypnotizer at her.

'What're you doing?' Margo asked, taking her eyes off the road ahead to glance sideways at him.

'I'm increasing the power to make sure she stays under the influence until she stops. Then I'll get the chance to give her the proper commands – to make her join our show.' Then he realized how Margo was driving the van. 'But don't *do* that! Don't *look* at me when I'm talking, just *listen*! Watch the road . . . !'

Margo's inattention at the wheel made the van zig-zag worse than ever. It took the full width of the street, from pavement to pavement, causing everything else *on* the road – to get *out* of the road!

And with all the zig-zagging about it wasn't just Super Gran who was being hit by the sound-waves – lots of innocent passersby were too! And, as Mystico was talking to Margo while speaking into the Hypnotizer, the passersby were, as usual, obeying his instructions.

'Stop moving about,' he told Margo. So the 'zapped' pedestrians stopped moving about on the pavements! 'Go straight,' he told her. So the pedestrians walked straight – when they *should* have turned, and they bumped into shops, trees and other pedestrians!

The procession through Tarborough continued: Super Gran on her skateboard, followed by Mystico and Margo, who'd now dropped back behind her again; followed, a fair distance behind, by Willard on his bike; followed – an even greater distance behind! – by Edison on *her* bike. And Super Gran led them through – and bumpily over! – the narrow cobbled streets which twisted downhill towards the harbour. And the tide was in!

If Super Gran went over the edge of the harbour what would happen to her? She was now fully under the influence of the Hypnotizer at its highest power, and couldn't stop herself. And there was no one else who could stop her. And there was no*thing* else to stop her as she came out of the last of the cobbled streets and into the broad, open space of the harbour. She crossed the harbour street, on to the quay – heading straight for . . .

'The edge! She's going over the edge!' yelled Margo, while Mystico shrieked:

'Brakes . . . !'

'I don't think skateboards *have* brakes!' Margo shouted back at him.

'No! Not the skateboard's – the van's brakes! Put on the brakes – the brakes – now . . . !'

Mystico, knowing what his van's brakes were like, knew that Margo should be applying them *now* – if she wanted to stop the vehicle before it went over the edge of the harbour . . .

Super Gran, if *she* went over the edge of the harbour, might drown, and Mystico needed her in his act alive, not dead. But, on the other hand, when she hit the water the Hypnotizer's effect would be cancelled, as had happened in Slackpool with the meter-maid. In which case Mystico would have gone to all this trouble for nothing, and would have to hypnotize her all over again!

But either way there was nothing he could do about it just then, from where he sat, helpless and terrified – biting his nails – in the van as it crossed the harbour behind Super Gran. For they were both, at that moment, heading straight for the edge of the quay and the water below . . . !

14 Harbour Horrors

While Super Gran was sailing through the air and Margo was bumping the van across the harbour, Willard was taking a shortcut through a couple of back alleys which led directly to the waterfront . . . while Edison was still cycling along, half a mile farther back!

Super Gran flew off the skateboard, sailed through the air – and landed, luckily, in a rowing-boat moored to the quay, full of ropes, nets and lobster baskets – which fortunately broke her fall.

Margo screeched the van to a halt – less than half a metre from the edge! – and it took several minutes for their nerves to settle before she and Mystico could think of emerging from it. Then Mystico, Hypnotizer in hand, leapt out and ran to the edge to see what had happened to Super Gran. He was worried. He didn't want to be had up for murder, after all! But then he relaxed, seeing that she was safe – and, better still, still hypnotized!

'Whew!' He breathed a sigh of relief, but swung round on hearing Willard's shout as the boy came bouncing on his bike out of a cobbled alleyway into the broad harbour area – and saw what was happening.

'Hey! What've you done to my Gran? Leave her alone, you big bully . . . !'

Willard cycled across the street to the quay and then, as he approached Mystico, threw himself sideways off the bike at the man. The riderless bike, meantime, went careering on in the direction of Margo as she walked towards him round the back of the van.

'Hey! Look out! Ouch!' she yelled, as the bike made contact with her.

Willard knocked the Hypnotizer out of Mystico's hands, but at the same time the collision broke the strap on his CB radio container and both objects fell on to, and rolled inside, a large coil of rope lying on the quay, which broke their fall.

Willard and Mystico grappled with each other while Margo, unwrapping Willard's bike from around her neck, sprang forward, stuck her hand inside the rope-coil and retrieved the Hypnotizer. Then, while Mystico and Willard continued to wrestle and roll about together on the quayside, she tried to aim it at Willard – trying *not* to hit her boss as she did so!

'Hold still, can't you?' she said in exasperation as they rolled back and forward on the ground. 'Look! I'm going to hit the wrong one if you don't hold still . . . !'

Meanwhile Super Gran, sprawled out in the rowing-boat, had a daft, glazed, hypnotic look on her face and was oblivious to what was going on above her, on the quayside. 'Where *am* I? Cromwell's Mount?' she mumbled dreamily.

By now Edison was arriving at the harbour. She saw what was happening on the quay – although she didn't, of course, see Super Gran in the boat – and decided to jump off her bike and throw herself at Margo.

When she did, two things happened. Firstly: the Hypnotizer was knocked out of Margo's hand and fell inside the coil of rope again – which broke its fall, again. And secondly: the jolt of the collision knocked Margo off-balance and she staggered to the edge of the quay – and fell over!

'He-elp . . . !' she yelled as she landed in the back of a speedboat setting out for a trip round the bay, driven by a handsome, blue-eyed, sun-bronzed young man.

Edison, too busy to notice Margo's disappearance, grabbed the Hypnotizer *and* Willard's CB radio container out of the rope-coil, while Mystico at last managed to break free of Willard's limpet-like clutches.

'Get off!' he growled at Willard. Then, jumping to his feet, he made a grab to recover the Hypnotizer from Edison. 'Gimme that . . . !'

But Edison thought quickly. Having put both objects behind her back, automatically, to hide them, she now switched them over and brought out only the radio container – which she allowed Mystico to grab from her.

'Got it!' he yelled triumphantly – but mistakenly!

The container was approximately the same size, shape and colour as the Hypnotizer, so it took a mystified Mystico a few moments to realize he had the wrong object. And while he was fiddling about with it, staring at it and trying to find controls on a blank radio container where none existed, Edison got to work! She carefully aimed the *real* Hypnotizer at him and put him under

its influence, but without actually giving him any commands to obey.

And, as its control knob was still at its highest, strongest setting – for hypnotizing Super Gran – it hypnotized Mystico rather too strongly. He ended up as stiff as a statue, and Willard's radio container slipped from his rigid, senseless fingers to the ground. It burst open and the radio fell out, unnoticed by Willard.

'That's got him!' the boy yelled in triumph, as he picked himself off the ground and saw the dazed, hypnotic look on Mystico's frozen face. 'Well done, Ed!'

'Eh? What? You actually praised me? You said something *nice* to me?' She was stunned, then recovered. 'But where's Super Gran?' There had been no sign of her since Edison reached the quay, and she couldn't understand it.

'She's over there somewhere – I think!' said Willard, forgetting about his radio as he led Edison to the edge of the quay. Although even *he* wasn't sure where she'd got to.

They looked over and saw that Super Gran was sitting dreamily amongst the nets, ropes and baskets in the rowing-boat and was still obviously under the Hypnotizer's spell.

'Cromwell's Mount ... skateboards ...' she murmured.

'At least she's safe,' said Edison. 'But she's still hypnotized.'

'Mystico was still doin' it to her while they were chasin' her in the van,' Willard explained. 'I saw him.'

'The wee scunner!' said Edison. 'Whatever *that* is!'

'Come on,' Willard said, 'let's *un*-hypnotize her.' And he put his hand out for the machine.

'It's all right, *I* can do it,' Edison replied haughtily, drawing the Hypnotizer back. 'It's *my* Dad's invention, after all . . .'

'Well hurry up then, it doesn't matter *whose* Dad's invention it is! Just get on with it!'

'Okay, okay. Don't nag!' said Edison as she pointed the Hypnotizer at the dizzy-looking Super Gran in the boat and pressed the reversal button.

Super Gran 'woke up' and looked all round: first of all at the rowing-boat she was in and the gear she was sitting amongst, then up at the quay above her, at Willard and Edison peering anxiously down at her. 'What . . . ? Where am I . . . ? What am I doing here?' She pushed her tammy aside to scratch her head, puzzled.

The last thing she remembered was racing Reg, on skateboards, down Cromwell's Mount. And the next thing she knew she was sitting, rocking gently with the tide, in a rowing-boat in the harbour! She was all at sea!

Then she spotted the Hypnotizer in Edison's hands and realized that that had had something to do with it. Mystico must have hypnotized her, and Edison had *un*-hypnotized her. She scrambled to her feet and climbed the ladder attached to the harbour wall, up on to the quay to join Willard and Edison.

'What's that?' Edison asked, as all three of them swung round to the sound of a siren. 'Is it the police?'

A panda car came shooting out of the narrow cobbled street and crossed the broad harbour area to the quay. It screeched to a halt on some loose, spilled gravel which was lying on the ground beside the trio, the statue-like Mystico, his van, the coil of rope, Willard's forgotten CB radio and container, the two discarded bicycles and Super Gran's skateboard.

The police had had a report about Mystico's van being driven recklessly through the town and causing a disturbance and they'd followed the trail to the harbour to arrest him. A sergeant and a constable climbed out of the car and approached the four people standing on the quay: Super Gran and Willard, Edison, clutching the Hypnotizer – and Mystico, standing still like a resting robot awaiting activation.

The sergeant sauntered towards the group, reached the motionless Mystico, snapped his fingers in front of his staring, unblinking eyes, got no response from him and said: 'Cor! Strike me! Stone the crows!' Then, scratching his head in a distinctly puzzled manner, he proceeded in an easterly direction towards Super Gran and company, near the edge of the quay. 'Now then, now then, what's all this about, eh?' he asked, gesturing, with a thumb, over his shoulder at the immobile magician.

'That's Magic Ian!' Willard informed him with a broad grin.

'Magic who?'

'He means – it's Mystico, the magician,' Super Gran explained.

'Make up your minds,' the sergeant grumbled, while the constable produced his notebook and pencil and wandered round Mystico's van, inspecting it and noting all its many faults for prosecution purposes.

Willard, with some help from Edison, told the sergeant that Mystico had used the Hypnotizer on Super Gran during the race and while pursuing her in the van through the town. Then he and Edison told him of the struggle they'd had on the quay with Mystico and Margo, and how they'd recovered the Hypnotizer from them.

'Hey! That reminds me!' exclaimed Edison. 'I'd forgotten all about Margo! I wonder what happened to her?'

She hadn't seen Margo landing in the speedboat and being whisked off in it and she wondered if she'd landed in the water, or perhaps, like Super Gran, in a moored boat. So she left the others and walked a few metres along the quay, looking over the edge to find out.

The police sergeant was amazed at the whole story. 'What? A hypnotizing machine? Cor! Strike me! Stone the crows!' He pushed his cap back to scratch his head. Then he called across to his constable: 'Take charge of the van, Jack. Run it in. I'll take chummy here back to the nick in the panda ...' He gestured towards Mystico as he spoke.

'Okay, sarge,' Jack said, putting away his notebook and pencil and climbing into the van to reverse it away from the edge of the quay.

'And you say that little gadget can hypnotize people?' the sergeant went on. He turned to see where Edison had got to with it, putting his hand out for her to return and hand it over for him to inspect.

'You know, laddie,' Super Gran said to Willard, as Edison walked back towards them with the Hypnotizer, 'this must be the first time ever that one of Mr Black's wee gadgets has survived one of our adventures!'

But she spoke too soon! For something *did* happen to it! But what *could* happen? For Edison, after all, only had to walk a few metres back to the others and hand it over to the safe custody of the police sergeant. So what could happen in *that* distance? Did she trip – as usual?

No, she *didn't* trip! She slipped – on an old, wet, slippery fish which had been left lying about on the quay!

'Oh no! Catch it, someone!' she cried as she landed on the skateboard, which shot off and carried her along the quay!

The Hypnotizer went flying out of her hand, up into the air. But it was all right, for three people went diving after it, to catch it.

Willard made an attempt, as if fielding a cricket ball – but he tripped over the coil of rope lying on the quay, and *he* ended up – lying on the quay! Then Super Gran made an attempt, but she was still a little bit woozy from the effects of the Hypnotizer and she tripped over Willard's discarded bike, and *she* ended up lying on the quay! And then the sergeant tried to catch it as it landed, but he tripped over *Edison's* discarded bike, and *he* ended up lying on the quay!

The sergeant, admittedly, got nearest to the Hypnotizer. He came within a finger-tip of catching it. The trouble was, his finger-tip accidentally tipped the operating button and his mouth came close to the microphone as he exclaimed, as usual: 'Cor! Strike me! Stone the crows . . . !'

The motionless Mystico got mobile. He came to life and obeyed the sergeant's commands. He struck him!

'Ouch!' the sergeant yelled, cupping his newly thumped nose in his hands. 'Ouch! By dose . . .!'

Then Mystico proceeded to pick up some of the loose gravel from the quay and, as there were no crows available, he threw it at some passing, surprised, seagulls!

But Super Gran and company didn't notice Mystico's assault on the stunned sergeant and the stoned seagulls. For they'd all been watching in horror as the Hypnotizer landed on the quay – to see how badly damaged it would be. But the damage was total! For it landed directly in front of the wheels of Mystico's van just as Jack, the police constable, was driving it away!

'Oh no!' exclaimed Edison, referring to her Dad's smashed Hypnotizer.

'Oh no! I spoke too soon!' exclaimed Super Gran, referring to her earlier comment about the Hypnotizer surviving their adventure.

'Oh no!' exclaimed Willard, referring to his CB radio – which he'd just put his foot on and smashed as he tripped over the coil of rope.

'Cor! Strike *be*!' said the sergeant through his sore nose.

He was thinking about everything he'd just witnessed: about the Hypnotizer getting smashed, about the seagull 'crows' getting stoned and about being struck by the hypnotized Mystico. But 'strike me' – or even 'strike *be*'! – was the wrong thing to say. For Mystico obeyed his command again – and again he struck him, this time on the chin.

'Right! That does it!' With a bellow of rage, the sergeant went for Mystico, who turned and fled across the quay towards Jack, who had stopped the van and was climbing out of it.

Just then a certain speedboat pulled into the harbour and cut its engine. And if Margo, its passenger, had looked up at the quay, she would have seen her boss, Mystico, dashing across it – pursued by a police sergeant, a police constable, Super Gran, Willard and Edison – who was just about to slip again on *another* old, wet, slippery fish!

But Margo didn't see *any* of this, for she was too busy gazing into the pale blue eyes of the tall, dark, handsome, sun-bronzed young boatman! And from now on Mystico was her *ex*-boss and all her ambitions of having a stage career as a pop-singer or a TV or film star – were over. Her only ambition was to stay in Tarborough to be near a certain boatman. For Margo was in love . . . !

THE GHOST AND BERTIE BOGGIN

Catherine Sefton

Bertie is the smallest Boggin in a house full of Boggins. Teased by his older brother and sister, he escapes to the coalshed where he makes a very special friend – a ghost who happens to know Florence Nightingale!

MR BROWSER
AND THE BRAIN SHARPENERS

Philip Curtis

Mr Browser and the whole of Class 8 at Chivvy Chase School fell under the evil influence of the alien Brain Sharpeners. Michael Fairlie alone escaped the treatment and he watched aghast as his classmates became obsessed with learning and homework – because Michael was the only person who realized that the Brain Sharpeners' plot threatened not only Chivvy Chase School but the whole world!

FANNY AND THE MONSTERS

Penelope Lively

Fanny Stanton is of the opinion that being the eldest of eight children is bad – but being a girl is even worse! Here are three delightful stories about the irrepressible Fanny, who is expected to lead the life of a demure Victorian girl but whose spirit and sense of adventure constantly lead her into trouble of one sort or another.

DOG DAYS AND CAT NAPS

Gene Kemp

Ten stories about animals – and their human owners. Cats and dogs are particularly prominent, but mice, gerbils and other assorted animals also weave their way through this delightfully offbeat collection.

JEFFY, THE BURGLAR'S CAT

Ursula Moray Williams

Nobody who saw Miss Amity and her cat, Jeffy, walking to the shops each day would have believed that the little old lady was a burglar. Only Jeffy knew the terrible truth and he was determined to reform his wicked mistress. But all Jeffy's efforts were foiled when Miss Amity took in a stray kitten, Little Lew, who turned out to be the perfect partner in crime ...

THE REVENGE OF SAMUEL STOKES

Penelope Lively

What on earth was happening on the new housing estate? Washing machines smelling of roast venison, tobacco smoke coming out of television sets, greenhouses turning into Greek temples ... It was enough to make Tim and Jane think that a malign spirit was at work!

Heard about the Puffin Club?

. . . it's a way of finding out more about Puffin books and authors, of winning prizes (in competitions), sharing jokes, a secret code, and perhaps seeing your name in print! When you join you get a copy of our magazine, *Puffin Post*, sent to you four times a year, a badge and a membership book.

For details of subscription and an application form, send a stamped addressed envelope to:

The Puffin Club Dept A
Penguin Books Limited
Bath Road
Harmondsworth
Middlesex UB7 ODA

and if you live in Australia, please write to:

The Australian Puffin Club
Penguin Books Australia Limited
P.O. Box 257
Ringwood
Victoria 3134